the one that got away

a novel

j. michael iddins

Editors:
Dani Carter Iddins
Misha Fletcher

Cover Design © 2021 Kim Lyon Design

ISBN: 979-8-218-35291-2

DISCLAIMER: Any similarity or resemblance of the characters in the following tales to any persons, living or dead, sacred or profane, is entirely coincidental, and might as well be taken as a sign from God. All characters and events – even those inspired by real people – are entirely fictional and are the product of the author's imagination. The names and places are made up, but the problems are all too real.

"...America...I'm sick of your insane demands...Your machinery is too much for me...There must be some other way to settle this argument... My mind is made up there's going to be trouble...I have mystical visions and cosmic vibrations...

It occurs to me that I am America. I am talking to myself again..."

-Allen Ginsberg

table of contents

the one that got away

townie life

There is one female who stands out among those long hours and numerous battles stretched across my youth. She stands out, not because she was a raving beauty. Not because she was an intellectual powerhouse. Not because she was a social butterfly. No temple will be built in her name. And when she returns to dust, even the dust may be heard to utter a sigh. Waverly was all-the-more-notable for the things which she wasn't. A negative description perhaps suits her best....but I will attempt to tell you, in positive terms, what she was...How shall I introduce her...how can I convey the gravity of her identity?

...Well, after years of thinking upon it, I can safely say that the spirit of the town had crystallized in this girl. So much did she embody the essence of the town that she and the town eventually merged in my mind. Some might say she was possessed by the town. Others might suggest that she was the walking, talking personification of the town. However one chooses to see it, her scars are still etched upon my frame...

Waverly's deep brown hair was often unkempt, and often flaunted its frayed, split-ends. She let the wispy tresses fall across her face, obscuring her brown eyes, as if seeing something and seeing nothing were equally preferable. A baggy orange Nirvana t-shirt clung to Waverly's curves, advertising a bliss that was never to be. The wardrobe breathed a long history of cultural appropriation, inhaling the novel and exotic, and exhaling a pale shell of the original, hollow and devoid of substance.

She sported billboards along her roadside, recruiting youth for an army, in an empire that had long since forgotten her. Someone once asked, "Why do they always send the poor?" I can tell you they do so because desperate folks will take desperate measures.

Waverly wore loose-fitting bell-bottom jeans, which gripped her pale thighs and fell away, toward her awkward flat-soled Airwalk shoes. She had begun shaving her legs at thirteen, like her migrained mother, because that's simply what was done. The tapwater bore her young hair down the drain, on a bed of fragrant foam, through the aging pipes, to merge and marry with all the other town waste underground.

Waverly's streets were lined with cracking paint and chipped brick facades, abandoned storefronts and shadows of tradition...locations killed by corporations and convenience. Waverly's footfall was silent as she walked, staring down at her pimpled, pothole streets, knowing she had nowhere else to be other than where she was. This predicament met her at every turn. How could she not become jaded and bitter?

Waverly hadn't the strength to contain a rushing river, though she liked the thought of rushing rivers. They excited her.

Instead, she was given a babbling brook, which she tucked shyly, almost shamefully, among her structures and sparse vegetation. On the northside of this muttering stream sat her park of deathstones, which protruded absurdly from her face at various angles, strange crooked teeth of time, whose worn and weathered surfaces hung between her lips. Into this yawning mouth of Waverly the townsfolk were routinely fed. In my time with Waverly, I would look on in horror as she chomped away at many a townie life.

School busses ain't sexy, but that's precisely where Waverly first made her move on me. My parents had rented a brown, run-down two-story house near Waverly's tracks, in preparation for a large home that would be built northwest of her conglomeration of crumbling structures.

When I was whisked away from Nashville and brought up north to Waverly, I couldn't have foreseen the burnmarks she would leave upon my brain. I couldn't have foreseen the number of scathing lashes she would set upon my skin.

My father had accepted a bigger, better deal for his construction expertise "up north" than he could get in Nashville. While he would drive a half hour to the nearest city every day - Mount Comfort, my mother would be lured into Waverly's countryside through her romanticized view of the rural, small-town life. She slipped on those rose-colored glasses, while my father attempted the impossible: to play the leading role in her fictitious small-town, one-act play.

I felt my mother was trying to slake her desire for a slower, simpler time... Before several miscarriages, finally a son, and then the complications of adult life. I was not consulted in these decisions. Why should I have been? All the youth must come to terms with our fates, being at the mercy of parental whims. We either resign ourselves to these circumstances, fight them, or embrace and use them to our advantage.

My family settled into the "cozy" rental, shag carpet, carpenter ants, and all. I was headed off to the local version of those great social sorting centers: Waverly High. I was less than thrilled by this new twist of fate, but recorded music flowed up wires from the device in my pocket and into my head, easing my introduction to Waverly, masking my new world with melodic enchantments. My coarse dark hair was pulled back in a ponytail. She looked up from behind the dark green pleather seatback, where she had been contemplating the torn and threadbare denim stretched across her knees. I climbed through the collapsible doors and made my way further up into that yellow and black schoolbus.

Waverly's hair was half-wet and half-dry from her morning shower. She combed some strands out of her face, and we locked eyes. The eyes of Waverly, at that time, were still half-full of that careless youthful laughter, which she would gradually pour out over the years. Her green eyes were sprinkled with flecks of knowledge gleaned from her brief time in a small world. On that particular day she wore an oversized Blind Melon concert T, and baggy jeans. She slid over near the window of that mobile yellow box, making room for me in the seat. I flashed a smirk of understanding, removed my headphones, and slid onto the leathery green surface.

Waverly now sat with her back to the outside world, arms up on both seatbacks. Surely, she could feel the cold steel of the bus against her arched back. She faced me squarely, suspiciously, inspecting this newboy. A bit of drool formed at the edges of her mouth.

A roughly-braided hemp cord dangled from her neck. On this twine swung a blown-glass pendant, encasing a smiley face, with tongue lolling stupidly out, and x's for eyes. The charm swung with the motion of the bus, as if keeping time, coming to rest between her two braless and pendulous breasts. Why time was kept in such a place, I'll never know. Perhaps it was simply something to do, something which people felt religiously must be done. I gazed hypnotically down at this unlucky charm, and the cleavage in which it came to rest. The bus abruptly slowed to pick up another kid, and again my eyes came up to meet her mocking gaze.

"Waverly." she said, jerking her chin upwards, as if to indicate, "What's up?"

"Jay." I returned, evenly, still matching her intense stare.

As the bus bumped along, down Waverly's streets, she lured me in with talk of the classic rock which floated on the airwaves, like a siren on the isle of souls. I think it was Ozzy's "Shot in the Dark" that was playing that first day. In some ways, it seemed Waverly was younger than I, in others, she was infinitely older. I reached into my backpack, found the perspiring Budweiser bottle I had taken from the garage fridge. I gripped it with one hand and twisted with the other. "Psst" the bottle said as the seal released. I ducked down, brought it to my lips for a swig, and then came back up. I offered the brown bottle to her, which she accepted and gulped. The beer tasted like shit, but was a means to an end. Between the two of us, we polished off the rest of the bottle and I stowed it back into my bag.

As our bus pulled into formation among the other busses at the school, I produced a small half-dozen egg carton from inside my backpack, which contained three remaining eggs. I popped the top open and we stared at those three bleached ovals perched upright in the blue styrofoam. We exchanged mischievous grins. She turned and squeezed the two pressure-releases, easing the bus window down. I grabbed three eggs in my open palm.

"Duck," I prompted.

She ducked, as I flung the three eggs through the open window.

"Smack!" they said, as they met the closed window of the opposite bus.

Waverly glanced quickly over at the confused, cross-eyed stare from the boy across the way. His confusion shifted to disgust. She began to laugh maniacally, rocking back and forth, slapping the green vinyl seat.

I cracked up, and my sides started to ache from the attempt to control the laughter which flowed from somewhere deep in our bones. Tears formed at the edges of my vision. I wiped them away with the sleeve of my hoodie. I dropped the carton and kicked it across the bus floor, under the seats.

We heard the overhead speaker crackle before the bus driver's husky female voice echoed through the bus:

"Who did that? Who threw an egg at that bus?" she questioned, eyeing us all in her oblong rearview mirror.

We all straightened up. No one said a thing.

"Who threw an egg out the window?"

Nothing. Ahh, solidarity…The sheer absurdity of the situation washed over us - but that was how our teenage years began - absurdly. Some mornings, I brought beer from the garage fridge. Some mornings Waverly passed me a one-hitter packed with pungent herb. Our morning convos quickly shifted from the generalities of Black Sabbath and Faith No More to much more probing, penetrating, and personal questions.

"If you could only pick one fantasy, what would it be?" ...and such proddings.

Her directness was surprising, given her appearance, but I regarded her with interest and curiosity. Even then, I think I sensed that she was melting through the hands of time much faster than others, like a wax figurine too close to the sun.

In the evenings, Waverly and I often spent many hours in hushed conversation, she from beneath her down comforter and I from mine, our limbs spread out across our respective nests. Waverly's web of wires stretched out to pull me in, carrying insulated speech above the rooftops and treetops of the structures she held loosely in her hands.

For a time we were very close, using nightly electrical pulses to beseech estrogen, testosterone, and adrenaline to flow up out of their respective glands. We sought to conjure these hormones, actualize and embody them, so as to ride their mysterious energies down the bumpy road of adolescence. Under the influence of their heady draughts we felt awakened, enlightened, the way sunflowers follow the sun.

I never slept with Waverly during those days, though we often spoke of it. Occasionally, she would reach down, unprovoked and squeeze on my budding man parts. On other occasions, I would slide my young hands up her ill-fitting shirts to explore those gravity-laiden white hills, which would welcome many a visitor in the coming years.

Though our relationship waxed and waned in the years to come, Waverly always welcomed me with her strange mixture of delight, indifference, and occasional hostility. I attempted to steer clear of her when those sparks of intolerance shot forth from her hands. I grew wary of her bipolar outbursts.

Still, she was always in the background of my battles, pulling strings which seemed designed to trip me up, planting the landmines of my youth. Her name often appeared stamped across my struggles, like the erratic emblem of an artist who had not forgotten to sign her masterwork.

Waverly and I smoked together, laughed together, played together. We intermittently welcomed and fought each others' advances, living out the elastic tide of teenage years. We threw flaming glass bottles at passing trains, watching the glistening cocktail fragments rain down upon the spent soybean fields.

We pulled ears of corn from their stalks and flung them through the darkness at the headlights of passing cars. We listened for the thud of the ear reaching its mark, followed by the screech of tires and voices swearing at the darkness. Laughter noticed our utter disregard for consequences and overtook us in the fields, throwing us to the ground until our sides ached.

Waverly and I demanded attention from the larger world, which continued to pass us by. We spoke of futures that only one of us would come to see.

scatterfield ranch

So many names and faces flashed across my path through Waverly, only to be swept along, down her creekbed toward some unknown destination. This was not the case, however, with the Scatterfield boys. The Scatterfields were a unique bunch, a constant supporting cast during the Waverly years. Their ranch, south of Waverly and off the beaten path, regularly served as a refuge for us in those days. Off Rush Line Road, down a narrow, half-mile drive sat the ranch. If one had the windows down, as we often did, the frantic killdeer called out, protecting their nests along the grassline. As the gravel drive forked into a trident, the driver veered off to the left, around a clump of scrub trees toward the Scatterfield place. A split-rail fence guided the visitor onto the ranch proper, up to a pole barn and the double-door garage on the east end of the house. A firepit, ringed in fieldstone, lay off to the south, flanked by a picnic table, a bench swing, and several large stumps, which we used as seats at many a bonfire.

Red Scatterfield was the oldest of the bunch. He was a stocky, ginger-haired kid. He was the most persistent and practical of the bunch. Red partied hard with us on the front end of our days at Waverly High, but gradually got more serious as he began to think about the future. He was a good student, worked hard, and played harder.

Next in line was Nick Scatterfield. I became closest to Nick in those days, who was a Pisces like myself. Whether or not you believe in that shit, he and I both have those calm, watery, observant personalities. We were both idealists and dreamers. He sported a blonde, shaggy mop, parted down the middle, and sideburns like my own. I began smoking regularly with Nick, out back behind Scatterfield ranch, in a treeline which ran along the north side of their property.

One major way that Nick and I differed, however, was that he was naturally good at almost everything he tried. You could show him a picture of a mountain outcropping, or a gorgeous sunset. He could then reproduce the image down to the most minute detail with paint or pen. He was an incredible photographer and naturalist. His plant identification regularly blew me away when we ventured out on smoke-sessions in the trails of many a nature preserve or state park. Nick devoured books in those days, and is partially responsible for my obsession with books and ideas.

Nick's knowledge on almost any subject regularly set the stage for our bonfire banter and philosophical debate. Nick and I both played guitar, and would often jam together, recording hours and hours of meandering riffs and melodies. All this natural talent eventually became a curse for Nick, as he found it virtually impossible to venture down one specific path, so in love was he with almost everything.

On the other hand, Red and I were far more similar in the way that we had to work incredibly hard to acquire our talents and skills. Not much came naturally to us. We both also tended to be far more decisive than Nick. Maybe that has to do with us both being the oldest or only boys in our respective families? Who knows?

The youngest Scatterfield boy was Jack, who, over the years, went from being just an annoying kid brother to a regular member of our crew.

Red's blue monster truck was housed inside the pole barn on the Scatterfield ranch, along with a tractor, a welding shop, and many other curious accumulations. In the top rafters of the pole barn extended a makeshift attic space, plywood tacked down to a few rafters. We utilized this space as a regular smoke spot. Clusters of us crouched there under the ridgetop in a haze, which hovered before seeping out the ridgevents up into the sky.

Kathy, the mom of the Scatterfield boys was a medical transcriptionist who worked from home, out of her office in the walk-out basement. For the most part she left us to our own devices. The patriarch, Ben (aka Benderbeast), worked long hours at a local auto parts manufacturer. After days that dragged, troubleshooting robotics issues on the factory floor, he often returned to the homefront exhausted and ready to cut loose. In the evenings when we had just started our fires, his silver Chevy truck would roll up to the double door. We would slap a beer into his hand and offer him some munchies. He was one of the few adults in those days that treated us as real human beings. Around the fire, Benderbeast would recount for us stories of his time in the Navy, sailing the seven seas on behalf of the American empire, tales of general mayhem while in port around the globe. I soon realized that his tendency to have periods of intense focus, balanced by the need to cut loose and kill some brain cells, had deep roots in his experiences as a young sailor. Ben passed on his love of the water to his oldest son, Red, who bought a small sailboat, which we sometimes took out on the local reservoir. Stocked with snacks, weed, and beer, we could be seen carving across that man-made lake at break-neck speed, the hull of the boat about three-quarters out of the water. I learned all the basics of sailing from Red, who was a patient and practical instructor.

Benderbeast also told us tales of his wanderlust days. Once he had finished his term of duty with the Navy, he pocketed his Navy cash, bought a bike and minimal camping equipment, and then set off across the midwest, biking and camping and smoking some good grass along the way. He told us tales of spending time in the boundary waters of Minnesota, of biking along the Mississippi River bluffs down around LaCrosse, WI. It wasn't hard to see why Benderbeast was so much more relatable than my own parents, who always seemed so uptight, and so concerned about appearances. On the one hand, life was an unpredictable journey. On the other, it was a series of prescribed exercises through which we all must be led. I opted for the former. And, whenever I wasn't grounded, my home away from home was the Scatterfield ranch.

mass hypnosis

Four miles north of Waverly, stood the moderately menacing structure of a country church. Its only real menace, as far as I could tell, lay in the brutal contrast of the brick structure with the feminie fertility of the surrounding soybean fields. In design, the house of worship was a pale hillbilly shadow of the great Dark Age cathedrals. While it hinted at some former Eurocentric greatness, the design also gave a nod to what Bill Bryson has termed the "Fuck You school of architecture." It was essentially a brick fist with the steeple as its raised middle finger.

"Parish of Elizabeth Ann Seton," announced a gothic-lettered sign, somewhat ironically, near the pillared awning. Stained glass murals of Saint Beggar and other famous ascetics were sprinkled throughout the building for good measure. Menacing gothic statuary greeted the parishioners. If one didn't know any better, one might have assumed, upon entering, they were in the first circle of Dante's Hell - a weekly monotonous meeting of remembrance and recall, and poorly edited stories from the childhood of civilization. I met many holy and unholy spirits beneath that roof.

"Tuck in your shirt, Jay." Mom demanded, lest I look a slob before the townies and farm families in attendance.

I half-heartedly complied, starting at the front, and working my way to the back of my green Polo shirt. This tucking-of-the-shirt was my weekly ritual as we marched up the scarlet carpet of the wide center aisle, toward our regular seats - third or fourth pew from the front. Mom devoutly insisted on our weekly attendance at the Sunday "mass" of the church. While my father had a much more laid back approach to religion, early on, he had agreed to defer to my mother on religious matters, in order to keep the peace. Religion, for him, seemed primarily a social affair, while with her it all was very meta, carrying with it the weight of life and death.

The Scatterfields too were Catholic, though Ben and Kathy were much more relaxed about practice than my own mother. Whenever possible, I skipped out to Scatterfield Ranch on Saturday night, so as to have the option, rather than the requirement, of attending. The Scatterfields attended a much more artistic and cosmopolitan Catholic church on the northern outskirts of Mount Comfort, when they attended at all. Their cross was a sculpture of an ancient and twisted tree without its upper branches. Their Jesus looked as if he had met his end within the past week or so, blood and sweat dripping vividly down his brow from the crown of thorns, large railroad spikes piercing his muscular wrists and ankles. I mean, if you are going to do religion, at least look like you made an effort. Include some nuance.

On most Sundays, I went through the motions in that country church north of Waverly: Sit, stand, kneel... Sit, stand, kneel... like an animal in training, caged between those lacquered wooden pews, anchored in place. All the while, I criticized and critiqued the building and service in my head. I stared up at the bald priest, seated in his petty oaken throne, cloaked in a green or purple garment and raising his hands in blessing over the congregation. He was the simple peasant king of Waverly. Off-key, he chanted the scripted and half-memorized portions of the service. My favorite days were the masses when they busted out the thurible, a large incense burner suspended from a chain. The priest swung the thurible like a pendulum, this way and that, over the altar and congregation, adding an aire of drama and mystery to the whole show. That was the best, but it only happened on rare occasions.

I eyed the white angels, saints, and cherubs overhead, which were set against a light blue heavenly backdrop...painted in a lackluster imitation of Michaelangelo's original. I surveyed the lighted candles and the creepy statuettes mounted along the walls, depicting the Passion of Christ, one of the fundamental myths of the faith. These fourteen "stations of the cross" depicted each instance of suffering which Jesus of Nazareth had lived out on the last day of his life, leading up to his crucifixion by the Roman Empire.

When I took in such sights, I saw not the "Son of God" and "saving grace," but the consequences of holding unconventional beliefs and challenging the status quo. "My God, my God, why have you forsaken me?" he cried out in pain at the very end of these stations of the cross. Here was a guy who went around flipping tables, challenging the exploitation of the temple cult, and received the highest penalty both the empire and his religion could conjure up.

Those last words were a colossal question mark upon my young mind. The forsaken...I saw Jesus as a very potent example of the ways in which free thought is a threat to groupthink and tradition. He accumulated followers by preaching that the end was coming soon. One thing is certain - his world did end soon. The fall of the temple in Jerusalem was the end of the world for the Jewish people who knew no other way of life. Jesus stood in a long line of heretics. Socrates was another. Nick Scatterfield had introduced me to books on his apology before he was poisoned by the court in Athens.

I didn't think these men could be gods, but they did teach me a thing or two about the subject. I wouldn't worship such a one, but I could follow in their footsteps. I should have known then that things wouldn't end so well for me when

I broke ranks. I did believe that both Jesus and Socrates were inspired by, and protected by some Great Spirit, even if they had very different words for their experiences. It seemed to me that there were two conflicting characters alive in Catholic dogma. There was Jesus the teacher and freethinker. Then there was Jesus Christ, the man transformed into some sort of magical, mystical spiritual superhero. Either way, worship wasn't in the cards for me. I felt that Christians didn't have a monopoly on miracles and mystery. In fact, they weren't very good at recognizing either of those aside from two thousand year old tales. As Jesus himself said, "Let the dead bury the dead."

The robotic behavior of the church congregation vaguely terrified me. I think I sensed on some unconscious level it was a threat to my budding individuality. I watched the khaki and sweater-clad parishioners genuflect (kneel on one knee and make the sign-of-the-cross) in the direction the raised altar, obediently when entering the pews (benches).They filed mechanically out of the oaken pews when prompted, joining the "communion procession" to receive the "body and blood of Christ," the bread and wine. I did the same, in order to avoid confrontation and conflict with my mother. God, it seemed to me, was not at home in such a stuffy brick building, stained glass windows obscuring the natural world, not in a book filled with second and third-hand stories, but in nature where all the true seekers sought. I felt intuitively confident in the concept of God as some Great Spirit above and beyond all else. I thought there might be merit in the vague concept of spiritual protection, but the rest seemed a hodge-podge soup of absurd barnacles accumulated through centuries...The priest handed me the mass-produced wafer and I placed it on my tongue. "The body of Christ," he intoned reverently. The cardboardesque flavor disillusioned me even further. What shitty bread was this? I stepped over and washed it down with a sip from the community cup - a chalice of wine and water and backwash.

The strange coagulation of emotions and concepts generated by my Catholic church experiences directly led to my pursuit of sin, which seemed a million times more interesting than those washed up Sunday mornings with the medieval organ music and the off-key chants. If this was salvation, I was picking sin.

Alternative music, in particular, guided me down an alternative spiritual path. The record labels had ready-made solutions for rebels like myself. I began listening to bands like Glen Danzig, The Misfits, and Deicide. Tool, Pantera, and Spineshank, among others, provoked thoughts which challenged the norm... Marilyn Manson's Portrait of an American Family and Antichrist Superstar were in regular rotation as well, pointing out the hypocrisy that ran through the systems that constrained my world. I hummed these tunes to myself while going through the motions, biding my time.

After the service, parishioners gathered around collapsible tables on the front sidewalk, enjoying the ritual post-service coffee and doughnuts. Boxes of chocolate and sprinkle-covered doughnuts were slowly emptied as their contents were snatched up by hungry hands. Children chased each other, playing hide-and-seek among the established shrubs and trees of the grounds.

The tulips were in bloom. I took a walk while my parents chatted with other adults. I kicked at the pebbles as I strolled behind the church and lit a smoke. I gazed out at the treeline and clouds in the distance. What a strange world this was...I finished my smoke and then made my way back around the front of the building, where my parents were lost in conversation with a few of the elders, discussing a possible remodel of the building.

I motioned to them that I was ready to go. My dad held up a finger as if to say, one minute. I struck up a conversation with a girl that seemed a few years younger than I. She was standing by herself and appeared quite annoyed. In fact, she had what some would describe as "resting bitchface." She had these butterfly earrings and a slight southern twang in her voice. It turned out that she was feeling and noticing many of the same things as I.

My parents had already disengaged themselves from their conversation and had wandered across the two-lane highway that separated the church proper from the gravel parking lot and parish office. I told my new acquaintance that we would talk again soon, and ran off after my parents.

I was so lost in thoughts from my conversation that I was about to jog across the highway without even looking. I was on course to do just that. I had my right foot raised, ready to step into the road, when something urged me to look left. I pulled back just in time for an SUV, traveling at 60 mph, to fly right in front of my face. Time slowed down and I saw the faces of those inside, cringing and open-mouthed, sure that they were going to hit this kid. My heart raced. I stepped back from the highway onto the gravel shoulder, my hands on my knees, taking short frantic breaths.

It was as if Waverly was saying to me, I can take you whenever I want, Jay. And some Great Spirit had swooped in with, "Look left, son. I got you." I was significantly shaken by that close-call, and made a conscious attempt to live more in the moment. *Slow down. Be aware of your surroundings*, I coached myself.

the five-finger discount

My first major confrontation with law enforcement occurred at a large indoor mall in Mount Comfort. My family had just moved into our newly-constructed home north of Waverly. Being out of the shitty rental, I began to put more distance between Waverly and myself. Since the Scatterfields lived significantly south of Waverly, closer to Mount Comfort, we often ventured into the city rather than spend time in Waverly.

One Thursday evening, Nick Scatterfield and I decided to take a trip down to the mall, to exercise our idle hands, which didn't have shit else to do. Nick's blonde hair fell across his eyes, as he smirked to himself. He was constantly chomping on gum, which he worked nervously between his tongue and teeth. He and I zig-zagged through the silent rows of parked cars leading up to the north entrance of the mall. The early sunset of mid-fall sunk below the buildings as we stepped indoors.

We began tossing out ideas for how to kill time, for she absolutely must be killed, we assumed. Wasn't that what people did? Should we go harass some innocent bystanders? Should we try to pick up girls? Should we go hang out in the food court? Eventually, it was decided that we would go on a shoplifting spree.

Lifting items from stores started years earlier for me, when I snagged a pouch of chewing tobacco for a neighbor kid who was a few years older than I...so desperate was my desire to be accepted... From that first grab onward, I enjoyed the thrill of the adrenaline coursing through my veins, the uncertain circumstances under which any theft occurs.

While I didn't feel right about stealing the belongings of individuals, I had no qualms about stealing from Corporate America, which seemed to operate in some kind of vague amoral haze anyway.

The spree began slowly enough. We hit a candy shop. I snagged a rolled package of Spree candies, just to be ironic. We hit a Sunglass Hut for some shades...A few other one-stop shops. Grab-and-go...grab-and-go...As we became more bold, things escalated quickly. We swam smoothly through the shoppers and the jazz which curated the shopping experience.

We decided to rent a red locker for a few quarters, to hold all the loot we were collecting. After each spot we hit, we went back to unload. This process continued for the better part of two hours. We hit a nature products store. We hit Hot Topic, loading up our bags with stacks of t-shirts and baggy pants. We hit Spencers, walking out with posters, suggestive nic-nacs, and other large items, right under the nose of the oblivious, underpaid clerks. The posters were the most awkward merchandise to snag, but they slid easily up into our sleeves as we reached further into the poster bin.

We were at the point where our locker was so full it would hardly close. I looked at Nick, as he shut the door to the locker, and brushed his shaggy hair from his eyes.

"Tunes," I stated, nonchalantly. "We don't have any tunes."

Nick pointed at me, as if to say rhetorically, "Good call, bro."

We headed toward Sam Goody, in the lower level of the mall. I had been lifting records for years at that point. I may or may not have been part of the reason behind the push to install censors near the entrances and exits of stores. At any rate, I had all the music I wanted at that point, so I decided I would snag a few Phish albums for Waverly, as an early birthday gift. I'm not sure what tunes Nick had decided to go for. He usually preferred Floyd or Zepplin, Petty or Kravitz. When we walked in, the salesman asked us if we needed help finding anything.

"No thanks," we said.

"We're just browsing."

The clerk nodded and went back to reading his magazine. This was our first mistake. We were the only ones in the store, save for maybe one other person. Secondly, the design of the store was wide open. There was no place to hide, no obstructions from view. It was a dumb, clumsy, and doomed effort from the start. Lastly, we shouldn't have walked in together. If we had arrived separately, one of us could still walk if the other got picked up.

I found the "Jam Band" section and flipped through to find "Ph". Nick wandered in another direction. I laughed under my breath for a minute as I contemplated the irony. I was Phishing. I found the album I was looking for and started to browse around further down the aisle, flipping through records periodically to feign interest.

As I bent over one section, I tried to pop the Phish from its protective plastic sleeve up into my shirt. Normally this was a smooth, effortless motion, but these plastic sleeves were not as pliable as the norm.

With one hand, I worked at the plastic sleeve, while I thumbed through records with the other hand. Record titles flashed in front of my eyes as I struggled with the Phish. I attempted one angle, and then another. I was determined, overconfident in my own abilities. But hard as I tried, this was one Phish that refused to be netted. There was a loud "POP." The store clerk looked up and squinted his hawkeyes in my direction.

I froze up. *Fuck*. This was a new and unprecedented turn of events. The store clerk swung around from behind the counter and moved swiftly in my direction, huffing and puffing self-righteously across the worn, patterned carpet.

"What do you think you're doing?" He asked rhetorically.

"I was leaning over to see this album here, and accidentally cracked the one in my hand," I muttered, half-heartedly.

I had to try something.

"We'll see what the camera has to say about that!" He spat.

"You too, son," he called out to Nick, who looked wistfully toward the entrance for a moment, but decided against a chase.

Here was the hawk-eyed conservation officer, picking me up for phishing without a permit, I mused, already somewhat removed from the situation at hand. As he grabbed us each by an arm, I tried one last time:

"Did you think I was trying to steal this, sir? I have more than enough money on me to pay for this record. Why would I steal it?"

He paused for a second, as if replaying the scene in his head. The plenty-of-cash part was true. A decisive look came back over his features and he tugged us toward the office at the back of the store. He wasn't taking the bait. He had clearly dealt with our kind before, and the camera was the ultimate arbiter.

The footage on the camera was, without a doubt, incriminating. We looked way more suspicious than I had thought. The stocky mallcop arrived shortly afterward. The manager and the heavyset mallcop questioned us, trying to figure out why we would steal when we had plenty of cash on us. Just keep your goddamn mouth shut, I thought to myself. Neither Nick nor I really knew what to say, so we kind of shrugged noncommittally. I didn't trust myself to say much at that point. The mallcop rose from the desktop where he had been seated, directing us toward the labyrinth of hallways which ran behind the stores in the mall.

"Wait," Nick stopped. "My coat, it's in one of the red lockers," he said, holding up the orange-handled key.

I stared at Nick in open-mouthed horror. The mallcop considered this for a moment.

"Allright," he said. "We can pick it up on the way out."

As we made our way through the concrete maze of halls, voices crackled across the mallcop's walkie talkie.

"You're taking the rap for all the swag in the locker," I whispered emphatically. "I wasn't going to mention it, but now you're leading the pig to the trough. You gotta learn to keep your damn mouth shut."

Nick stared at his feet dejectedly, like a wounded pup.

"Roger," he said, resigning himself to his fate.

When we reached the red bank of lockers, the mallcop motioned to Nick for the key. Nick hesitantly placed the key into the mallcop's bearlike palm. I shook my head, having already foreseen the outcome of Nick's blunder. As the mallcop swung the locker away from its latch, his eyes grew wide.

"What have we here?" He intoned dramatically.

He radioed for backup. Once another mallcop arrived to oversee the documentation and redistribution of the locker contents, we were marched through the mall, out to the officer's patrol car by the rear entrance of the mall.

"Hands over your heads," he commanded when we reached the waiting ride.

He patted us down, finding nothing of interest other than a lighter and some smokes. I made small talk with the cop, as we were placed against the cold steel side of the car and hands were cuffed.

"How long you been stationed at the mall?" I asked, curiously.

"Bout six years," he replied.

"You ever worked down on the south side of Mount Comfort? I hear it's rough down there." I queried. I had heard stories.

"Yes sir, Potomac Street is hands-down the worst part of town. You kids from the suburbs best stay up here on the north side. Was on patrol down there for a bit. Couldn't get off that assignment too soon."

"That's what I hear," I offered.

"You kids watch your heads now," he cautioned, as he ushered us into the back seat.

Nick was silent as the grave, letting his blonde hair fall over his eyes. I looked around at the dark blue plastic of the unpadded seat, which my jeans slid readily across. The cuffs were cutting into my wrists. I looked up and met the officer's eyes in the rearview mirror, through the wire mesh which separated the back seat from the front.

"Just out of curiosity, why no padding on the back seat?"

"Are you kiddin me son? How we gonna clean clean up piss and puke from a padded seat?"

"You pick up people who piss in this seat?"

"Hell yes, son. We see all kinds…"

I left it at that, watching the buildings pass as we turned away from the mall. So this was normal for some? Damn. What a strange existence. We passed the lazer tag place where I sometimes went. Parking lot was still half full. We passed the hockey arena. A sizable amount of cars there too. How strange. Some playing hockey and lazer tag, while others were getting cuffed and stuffed in cells...

Ultimately, I took the rap for the record, while Nick claimed responsibility for the loot in the locker. We were driven to the juvenile detention facility down the street, to await our parents. My mother came quickly, appearing disappointed and clearly shaken. I was grateful I didn't have to stay overnight in that filthy place. I eyed a lineup of young black kids, wondering what their story was. What brought them into this purgatory? Would this place soon become a hellish home-away-from-home to them, or would they make it out of Mount Comfort? An officer unlocked my cuffs and escorted mom and I out. I hesitantly left Nick cuffed to a bench in the lobby.

"See you soon bro."

I think I was grounded for several months after the incident. Nick wasn't so lucky. His mom, Kathy, left him at juvee overnight, to think about his actions, and contemplate where his life went wrong. I felt bad for him. I pictured him handcuffed to that cold steel bench. I felt bad for my parents too, but not bad enough...

In those days, as I have said, we worshipped adrenaline, and she cared not for the fallout of our actions. We were consequently banned from the Mount Comfort mall.

Some say that, "idle hands are the devil's workshop." I don't believe there is a "devil" in any literal sense, much less that he or she would be petty enough to employ fifteen-year-old boys. But had our time been better booked, such ordeals as the Mount Comfort Mall Incident may not have happened.

Having said that, I don't ultimately think the morality of the issue is as clear as we think. Is stealing from a group that occupies stolen land actually stealing? You might say that, "Two wrongs don't make a right." That's a fair point. But the waters do get murky, and morality does get more relative, depending on whose point of view is taken and how far back we go.

What ultimately causes more harm to a society, petty thieves or tax shelters? Betting the fortunes of others on the stock market or shooting dice on the corner? Can we really rely on the morality developed by a society based on land acquisition, money-hungry corps, and genocidal tendencies? Dubious, at best. I'm not going to sit here and justify our adrenaline-fueled teen actions. But at that age, we were swimming in the murky materialistic waters of Waverly and the mountain of comfort on which she sat.

llama, llama, marijuana

At some point early on, in my time at Waverly High, I began a morning ritual. I rolled out of bed every morning around 6:20. I tossed off my covers and walked sleepily into the bathroom, across the hall from my walkout basement bedroom. I flicked on the bathroom fan light. I had the only bedroom on the first floor, and I treasured the early morning peace and quiet. After emptying my bladder and flushing, I pulled up my sweatpants and reached down to remove the bottom vanity drawer from its track. With the drawer removed, I peered at the hidden contents of the cabinet - my tea stash - which consisted of several sandwich bags of weed rolled up into ⅛ and ¼ oz portions, ready for sale; a larger rolled bag of my personal stash; a small paperweight scale; rolling papers; a few cigars; and of course Blue Magic, my blown-glass pipe of swirling violets, greens, yellows, and oranges against a murky blue and charcoal backdrop. I greeted every single day with Blue Magic in hand, sending up burnt offerings to the gods of the morning and the hovering mist of the fields. I self-medicated in preparation for Waverly's daily onslaught.

I broke off enough sticky greenish-brown leaves from a bud in my personal bag to fill up Blue Magic's thumb-sized bowl. I packed the leaves gently down and grabbed a lighter from my cabinet stash. I returned the drawer to its track, gently closed it, and walked across the cured-concrete basement to the patio door. I silently twisted the brass locking mechanism, listening for the lock's well-oiled release. I eased the door open, swinging my lanky body out into the morning air. I left the door slightly ajar, snugging it up to the weatherstrip for good measure. I plopped myself down into the painted steel patio chair and took a deep breath of fresh air. Our puppy, Terra, bounded up happily to get some pats and sit at my feet.

I sparked up the leafy green substance in the belly of Blue Magic. There, on that small patio, I consulted with the Indiana country morning, gazing into her sleepy eyes to see what each day might bring. Once the contents in Blue Magic's belly were sent either up to the heavens or deep into my lungs, I made my way back inside, showered, and got ready for the day. This quiet and thoughtful routine was often juxtaposed with the adrenaline-filled days at Waverly High.

The Waverly mascot was supposed to be a warhawk, which was fucking ludicrous since most people didn't even know what a warhawk was (a WWII plane or a person who advocates agressively for war). Besides this fact, the mascot image looked more like a vulture than a hawk... This was just one small example of the web of absurdities that I navigated in my teenage years at Waverly High.

Most of my friends and I arrived at by bus. A few of my friends had cars, but I wasn't allowed such a privilege. My parents made it clear that I was on a tight leash. That metaphor should be at least a little illuminating. It was clear to me that my parents did not much differentiate between the tasks of training a pet and training their son. Person A completes process B, this leads to productive outcome C. Grey areas were foreign lands to the Chapparals.

Most mornings my crew would meet up by the Waverly trophy case, molded plastic reminders of her past "success." News of the day fluttered about us. More often than not, a handful of us would make our way back out to the parking lot and head to Archie's Sandwich spot for some breakfast. In those days, teacher's aides collected attendance slips from the classroom doors, so if you had an "understanding" with a teacher's aide, you could make sure your attendance was altered as needed. You were good to go. Because of this set-up, my friends and I racked up thousands of hours of false attendance records, either excused absences or notation of our ghostly presence when we were elsewhere. It was, essentially, a political microcosm. We filled these reclaimed hours with many adventures, which we tucked away from Wavery's prying eyes.

Our main arch-nemesis was a Waverly assistant principal who we dubbed Gordo, a Spanish reference to her size. She had frazzled blondish grey hair, with enormous eyeglasses on a neck chain. For her costume, picture, if you will, a christmas ornament brought to life. Whatever you are picturing is a fairly accurate representation of the foolishness with which we daily dealt. Walkie talkie in hand, she hobbled up and down the hallways, flashing forced and tight-lipped smiles, harassing the miscreants and troublemakers such as myself. I was permanently on her radar in those days, and ever attempting to evade the evil eye.

At one point, I was questioned about a stolen Rolex watch. I don't remember if I had actually stolen the watch or not, but one of my buddies vouched that I had borrowed it from him. The next day, I borrowed a watch from everyone I knew. I made sure that when my arms caught her evil eye, they were covered from wrist to armpit in flashy timekeeping devices.

What could she do? It wasn't against any rule to have more than one watch. It wasn't against any rule to borrow a friend's belongings. I had studied Waverly's rulebook from front to back.

Gordo, if it was possible, puffed herself up even more than normal. We watched as her brain short-circuited. If one would have stuck her with a needle in those days, all that hot air would have sent her sailing from one end of the school to the other, bouncing off walls and unfortunate students as she deflated. What puffed up Gordo more than anything was that we knew the student handbook better than she. We could quote pages, sections, and subsections. In my opinion, that was the most important document in the school.

If we took Gordo seriously at all, it was because she did have a modicum of positional authority. With Waverly's sanction, she could do actual damage to our lives and futures, if we let our guard down. Gordo's henchman was a man we referred to as the rent-a-cop. The rent-a-cop was similar in size to Gordo, and usually sat stationed just inside the main entrance to the building. You could tell how active the day had been for him based on how saturated his shirt was in sweat. On most days the rent-a-cop functioned more as a scare tactic than anything else. On those days there were noticeable emanations of sweat from the armpit regions, expanding slightly beyond. A pancake-sized circle along his lower back also indicated a slow day. When the sweat had snuck up past his mid-section, into the shoulder blade region, we knew it had been a busy day for the rent-a-cop.

On one particular day though, he almost took Nick Scatterfield down. It started on a mundane Indiana morning. Winter snuck away, leaving the cornfields of Waverly cold and grey. My guy Red Scatterfield and I had decided to head to Archie's, smoke, and then maybe visit the llamas south of Waverly. Red was as usual, aggressively chill about it, his long ginger hair pulled back behind his ears. His left eyebrow, which sported a barbell piercing, always scrunched up when he was about to get into some shit. He was two years older than Nick and I, but we were, nonetheless, on a level. When he wasn't working or wrenching on cars, he dabbled in running Cross Country.

Nick agreed to join Red and I on our excursion, but he had to go throw something in his locker first.

"Careful with that locker," I smirked, throwing some shade his way.

Nick smirked back and then turned to leave. Nick was an anomaly in Waverly, I reflected. He was, in my experience, the most stereotypical "stoner" I have ever met. He spoke like a California surfer, his speech slow and filled with "dude" and "bro". He had short, shaggy hair. He probably smoked even more Waverly's finest than me, which is really saying something for those days. Often the two took Red's blue monster truck to school, but occasionally they would take Nick's silver Chrysler. Often, when Red wasn't along for the ride, Nick rode around with a two-foot glass bong strapped into the passenger side seat belt. If ever we tried to ride shotgun in his car, he would motion us to the back, saying,

"No, bro. Move on back, move on back. You know that's American Woman's seat."

He was simultaneously the most knowledgeable, yet goofy fool I had the good pleasure to run around with. There was never a dull moment with Nick along for the ride.

Red and I told him we would grab the car and then swing around to pick him up at the main entrance. He was going to sign out with the rent-a-cop, saying that he was leaving for the dentist. Red and I headed toward the back of the school, exiting out some seldom-used northside doors by the gym. We propped the door with a bic pen, and then made our way through the sea of cars, over to the lonely old oak, near which Nick's Chrysler was parked.

Red and I climbed into the car. I carefully wrapped American Woman in a towel and moved her to the floor. In those days, Red was constantly pulling all that fiery hair behind his pierced ears. I always wondered why he didn't just pull it back into a ponytail. At any rate, Red started bumping some Beastie Boys - Brass Monkey - if I remember correctly. He adjusted his eyebrow ring, and threw the car in reverse. We backed out of the spot and headed toward the steel awning of the main entrance.

As we rounded the northeast corner of the building, we saw Nick come bursting out the double doors.

"Hit it!" I prompted.

Red stepped on the gas. I reached back and rolled down the rear window. We came speeding up to the main entrance, braking momentarily, long enough for Nick to throw himself through the open window into the backseat. Nick's upper half was in, but his legs still struggled wildly for the safety of the grey cloth backseat. Rent-a-cop was close behind, but Red pounded the gas again, and we were off to adventure, Nick's legs still flailing out the window as we turned onto the nearest country road. Once out of view, we slowed and Nick settled himself in the backseat, brushing his blonde hair out of his eyes, breathing out a sigh of relief, and clicking his safety belt buckle.

"Let's go see the llamas, bro!" Nick said, still breathing hard and throwing up his favorite hand signal, thumb and pinky finger up and the others folded in.

"I'm down," I shrugged, drumming on the armrest to the beat.

Red reached down and passed American Woman back to Nick.

"To the llamas," he grinned, starting to pack up the pipe.

There was something timeless and calming about the llamas, something which spoke to us of things that mattered way, way more than Waverly High. In a way, the llamas were our spirit animals, if you believe in that kind of shit. When we pulled up to the pine fence, they trotted up to meet us, slowly chomping fieldgrass in their masticating mouths. They stood near the fence, regal and alert, yet unconcerned in those pastures south of Waverly. It was rare that they wouldn't let us run our hands through their coarse fur. Sometimes their wide brown eyes met ours, while at other times they stared off, at nothing in particular. In the eyes of a stoned and rebellious kid, the calming presence of these creatures was preferable to instructors parroting words off a page. Nick was usually the first to break the silence:

"What the fuck is up, Llama! You like that grass? I had myself some grass today too bro! That's some good shit, right?"

"I'm just glad American Woman's along for the ride," Red suggested.

"Bro," said Nick, "American Woman had a close call. If it wasn't for the two of you, she would have been smashed upon the rocks!"

I thought back to the previous week's scare, when admin brought drug-dogs into the parking lot. Red and I received word that the cops had sniffed out Nick's ride. They were in the main office, questioning Nick. They would make Nick go out and unlock the car for them. Red and I rushed out into the parking lot, in a race against time. When we got to the car, Red didn't hesitate. With his right foot, he kicked in the passenger side window, sending glass shards flying every which way. He reached in and unlocked the door. Frantically Red and I combed through the car for anything even remotely damning. We grabbed American Woman, papers, lighters, a scale. We slipped back into the school, as quickly as we had come, sliding out of sight as the officers, dogs, a principal, and Nick came around the corner. Red and I watched from a window as the entourage came up to the car. The posture of the officers became more alert and they scanned the parking lot for signs of life. They began to go through the car. Nothing. We could see Nick gesturing dramatically. I imagined him saying,

"Bro, you busted my window out - not cool! You brought me all the way out here to show me how much you trashed my ride - not cool."

The confused adults went back and forth for a time, hands on hips, gesturing. They documented the vandalism, and then escorted Nick back to class.

"Let's thank our lucky llamas American Woman survived." I nodded toward the field and the peacefully chomping creatures. I ran my hand across its nose as it tried to nibble at my fingers.

Nick started imitating the facial expressions of the officers upon seeing the smashed window. We all burst out laughing.

"They were fucking baffled, bro. I wish you guys could have seen it!"

drive-in, drive-out

For some time, I dated an upperclassman named Megan. She was a tall, leggy volleyball player. I'm not sure how we even met each other, since we had none of the same classes. Perhaps I just approached her in the hall one day, walking out of the crowd into her life. Megan and I had a pretty steady relationship - no real ups and downs. One of our favorite dates was to do a couples movie night at the drive-in theatre between Waverly and the next small town, Groverton. At dusk, we would all pile into a car, and then head out of town, parking in the field which spread out before the giant billboard screen.

Megan and I had a fairly light-hearted relationship. I hadn't yet passed through any of the real struggles of my high school years, and she was a fun-loving, light-hearted girl. I remember our time together as one of the most sober times in my adolescence. Us couples would pin down our spots in the field. We would spread out some blankets on the close-cropped grass. Snacks and drinks were produced. We chatted and laughed for a time, until the movie started.

Once the sun was firmly set, and the previews began to roll, our hungry adolescent hands found each other. Not too long after one couple began the quiet kisses and heavy petting, the next was sure to follow. Nick and Hope usually started things off. Megan and I followed suit. In this manner, we explored the mysteries of budding sexuality under the cool night skies and the glow of moving pictures. For a time, this was our Friday night routine.

One added benefit of dating an "older woman" was that she had her license and owned a vehicle. I did not yet have either. We both had jobs, and no real bills, so we had plenty of disposable income to spend on our weekend adventures.

One Friday evening, we completed our drive-in ritual, as was typical. A cool, crisp fog blanketed the night. After the credits rolled, signaling the end of the experience, Megan and I slipped into her car and headed north on a state highway toward my house, out in the country. We talked and laughed as she steered down the smoky blacktop. The music was loud. I was teasing her about something, giving her shit. In the haze of our mutual infatuation, we forgot about the sharp s-curves on the highway. There we were, two love-drunk kids speeding through the foggy night.

"Look out!" I suddenly shouted, my body tensing up.

Before anyone could react, her white Buick launched itself from the road, into the fog. The car tore through the yellow sign which warned of a sharp curve. Megan tensed up and clenched down on the steering wheel. Her eyes grew wide, searching for solid ground.The speeding car flew over the ditch and landed hard in someone's front yard. We both had our seat belts on, thank God.

"Keep driving!" I shouted.

She hit the gas, tore through some poor man's garden, mowing over neatly staked tomatoes and fresh melons in the dark. Once beyond the garden, her headlights found the gravel driveway. She maneuvered the car onto the drive, and turned back onto the highway. The whole thing took place in a matter of seconds. Her face was tense with anxiety, her eyes still wide and alert. She combed her hair behind her ear. I started laughing hysterically, doubling over, and pounding my knee as the laughter came.

"You gotta warn a guy before you take 'em off-roading! Jesus Christ, Meg!" I managed.

She laughed a nervous laugh.

"You probably got veggies stuck in your grille!" I laughed, holding my fist to my mouth, as I often do when something gets good to me.

Gradually, the waves of laughter cut through her panic, and I watched her shoulders relax. She began to laugh as well, at first softly and then louder and longer. I reached for her hand, and we continued up and down the rolling hills, through the fog toward my parents' house. We ended that evening parked in my parents' gravel drive, staring into each other's laughter-filled eyes, which captured what little light there was in the darkness.

Unfortunately, the drive-in dates came abruptly to an end. Megan's parents were going out of town and our drive-in group decided to have a little get-together at her place. Oddly enough, I had never been into Megan's house, and she had never been inside mine. I think it just happened that our relationship centered around school and the drive-in. No one wanted the interference of parents at that point... In hushed tones, Megan and I spoke over the phone. She wanted that night to be the night she lost her virginity.

I had never slept with anyone before, but with hormones in full swing, I nervously made preparations for the big night. I procured some condoms, and she procured a few bottles of alcohol to steady our nerves.

When the night came, all started off as planned. The three couples showed up in her neighborhood as the sun set. We were directed down carpeted stairs, into the finished basement. Music flowed from wall-mounted speakers, and mood-lighting emanated from the recessed lights in the ceiling. Megan was throwing ice into red solo cups, and mixing drinks. We all drank and laughed for a bit, played a few games. After a while, one of the other girls motioned toward the bedrooms, at the far end of the basement.

"I think it's about time, Meg! You guys ready?"

Megan and I locked eyes. We were the only couple in our friend group that had not yet slept together. Nick and Hope were there. They cheered us on.

"What do you think?" I asked, feeling surprisingly hesitant.

She nodded nervously, biting her lip. I reached for her hand, and we walked toward the basement bedrooms. She intertwined her fingers with mine, and pulled me toward an open door on the right. Nick and Hope fell into the room on the left, Nick running his fingers through Hope's bright orange hair.

I won't go into all the details, but we guided each other through a nervous inaugural run that night, awkwardly unwrapping the condom and hesitantly proceeding as one does when they have no idea what they are doing. I don't think either one of us "came," but we had crossed a threshold, entered the club. At the time I had minimal knowledge of female anatomy and no real notion of foreplay. Uninformed teenage sex leaves a lot to be desired.

In the dim light, we could see beneath us a huge red stain spreading across the bed. She had not warned me she was on her period. Maybe she didn't know. We were both so ignorant...I didn't even have time to process. Suddenly, we heard the bass from a booming voice out in the main room.

"My brother! This is his room!" She sat up looking panicked.

I flung myself off the bed, and started pulling up my pants.

"What!? We just had sex on your brother's bed?!"

There was no time for discussion. We were both frantically clawing at our clothes. The door flew open.

"What the fuck?!" her older brother's voice boomed. His bulky frame stood in the doorway.

Nick and Hope emerged, looking stunned.

"Are you serious, Megan!?" Her brother grabbed me by the shirt, pushed me up against the wall, scowling down at me.

"I ought to kick your ass right now!" He threatened, through gritted teeth.

"No!" she said frantically. "It was my idea," she pleaded. "Let him go."

His grip on my shirt relaxed, and I pulled away.

"Get the hell out of my room, before I reconsider!"

Nick and I attempted to run and slip our shoes on at the same time, bolting up the stairs for the front door. We made it up through the front door, letting the storm door slam behind us as we made it out into the fresh air. We ran across the lawn to the Chrysler and peeled out, speeding past streetlamps down the block. I was sweating, thinking for sure I was dead. For sure that big mother fucker would second guess himself and come for me.

I worried about it for days, even after I spoke to Megan on the phone and she assured me that it was ok. She had told him we used protection. It probably helped that her brother was over 21. It would be assault if he came after me. Megan and I didn't last long after that. I would see her in the halls at school occasionally, but after that traumatic night, our chemistry began to fizzle and dissipate. We remained acquaintances, but walked in different circles.

I heard through the grapevine, from one of my female friends, that she was struggling with anorexia and bulimia for a time. That saddened me. I was pretty uneducated about such things at the time and just figured it would get sorted out over time. Years later I heard she had joined the military, in order to escape the fate of a life in Waverly. That was the last I heard of her.

The trauma associated with losing my virginity reverberated long past that night. I grew ever more cautious. I always knew I didn't want to be a young parent, so I wore raincoats whenever I was active. But from what I could tell, teenage sex was a bit overrated. It didn't live up to the hype. Too much fucking trouble

gym class zeros

Nick took a long, slow drag from the mouth of Blue Magic. He manned the carb with his thumb as the bowl sat perched in his right hand like a snug little bird. We sat shoulder to shoulder, halfway down a stairwell, which led between the weightroom on the second floor and the auxiliary gym on the first floor. The two of us sat facing down the linoleum-tiled staircase, away from the weightroom door, where the rest of the class was busy lifting.

I'd always told myself I'd never smoke at school. That was just flat-out stupid. But our boredom with the workaday world of Waverly High had reached a fever pitch. It was as if Waverly was attempting a slow lobotomy on us. These were the years just before every adolescent had a phone in their palm, salving their boredom and mesmerizing them with social media feeds. Finally, we decided to risk it. What other options did we have? Sit there and take it? Naw.

I took a sip from the white plastic water bottle which contained my daily dose of OJ and Dark Eyes Vodka. The stairwell was beginning to haze with the smoke which rose up from the glowing red eye of the glass bowl. Nick's lungs worked to fill up the glass chamber once more. He then removed his thumb from the carb, to empty the tiny chamber a final time. Nick brushed his hair out of his eyes. His squinted eyes were full of that foolish confidence and quirky pop-philosophy, downright schoolgirl silly. You couldn't be stoic or morose in the presence of Nick. He just emanated positivity and lightness of heart.

As Nick exhaled, smoke rings rose up into the otherwise vacant stairwell. Hazy O's floated up, and then gradually dissipated. I never could master those smoke rings Nick blew. He guardedly passed Blue Magic into my hands. I nodded my thanks as I cupped the bowl of swirling colors and took a hit.

"I can't think of a better way to spend gym class," smiled Nick through bloodshot eyes. "Really works the lungs."

I chuckled as I passed the water bottle to Nick, who took a long swig and passed it back.

"I always thought this stairwell would make a good smoke spot," I noted, scanning the spot and issuing a muted cough into my fist. I handed the glass piece back to Nick.

With the loud creaking sound of unoiled hinges, the door at the top of the stairs flew open. Nick and I stood straight up, but were careful not to turn around or reveal anything we held. Coach Corker's voice boomed from the top of the stairs:

"Well, well, if it isn't Jay Chapparal and Nick Scatterfield? Whatcha fellas doing? Takin' a lil cigarette break?" Corker paused and sniffed the air like a bloodhound…

"Wait now, that's not cigarettes, is it? That's marijuana. You guys been smoking marijuana in this stairwell?"

Corker was one of Waverly High's beloved teachers. Not only was he awarded teacher-of-the-year multiple times, but he had also led the football team to several state championships.

I piped up, "We haven't smoked anything. It stunk like that when we got here. I was trying to figure out what that smell was...I just had to talk to Nick here about something."

Corker chuckled to himself, and shook his head, like a seasoned detective that had just cracked a pesky case.

"Sure you haven't smoked a thing...because I am stupid…"

"You said it, not me," giggled Nick, quietly to me.

We erupted in laughter. That pissed off Corker, whose eyebrows furrowed and face grew stern. There was half a staircase in between Corker and us sophomores.

"What?" hissed Corker. "How about we take a little walk down to the office?" he asked, rhetorically.

"Sounds good," I shot back, "...that way we can clear up this misunderstanding. You like walks, Nick?"

"Yeah, I like walks," said Nick, giggling like a little girl.

In my left hand, I clutched the white water bottle close to my chest, and concealed a small zip-loc bag of green leafy vegetation in my right. Nick concealed the glass bowl in his right hand, which was now inside his pocket. The three of us began to make our way casually down the staircase, Corker from the top, Nick and I from the middle landing. I felt the screwdriver drink sloshing against the sides of the water bottle as I walked down the steps.

As soon as Nick and I hit the door at the base of the staircase, I rounded the doorway out of the staircase, expertly tossing the baggie of bud into the open end of a tall section of bleachers. I bolted across the polished wooden surface of the auxiliary gym. Seeing me take off in a sprint, Corker took off in pursuit. By the time he made it to the base of the stairs, I was halfway across the aux gym, and had already ditched the bag of bud. Nick giggled as he watched my skinny frame fly out the double doors of the aux gym and round the nearest corner, the stocky frame of Corker struggling to gain on me. Calmly, Nick walked over to an open janitor's closet at one end of the aux gym, and tucked Blue Magic under a long floor-broom, where it would be safe until he could send someone back for it or come back for it himself. Then he set off calmly in the direction of the chase.

I rounded the painted cinder block corner out of the aux gym at a full sprint, past a line of confused students. Corker was breathing hard, trying to close the gap between himself and I. My stick legs pumped hard, my baggy Jnco pants flapping in the wind. I rounded another corner, past the empty concession stand and into the main gymnasium.

I caught the white cinder block corner with my right hand and swung myself into the boys' locker room. Frantically, I spun the lid off the water bottle containing the mixed drink. I splashed the rest of its contents onto the wall just above the nearest trash can. Orange juice and vodka ran down the wall, and out of sight. I tossed the empty water bottle into the open-mouthed brown trash can and sprinted over to the nearest urinal. By the time Corker huffed into the locker room, I had my pants unbuttoned and was beginning to urinate.

"What the hell is wrong with you, Chapparal?" Corker panted between breaths.

I knew Corker couldn't lay hands on me until I had finished. I looked back over my shoulder calmly at Corker, who stood glaring at my back, hands on his hips.

"God, I had to piss! I thought I was going to piss my pants! You can imagine how embarrassing that would've been!"

Corker shifted his weight, fuming.

"You gotta be kidding me, son..."

I finished, zipping up my fly and buttoning my pants.

"You've never had to piss that bad?" I eyed Corker, smiling hautily.

Corker just shook his head knowingly as I walked over and washed my hands. I pulled a brown paper towel off the James River towel dispenser and, drying my hands, continued:

"Alright, coach. Let's head on down to the office."

As Corker and I walked out of the boys' locker room, Nick rounded the corner calmly and joined us.

"Hey Jay, have to piss?" asked Nick, in mock concern.

I nodded.

"Something terrible, man."

"I know how that is…" said Nick giggling to himself.

Nick and I were escorted silently past the glass-enclosed trophy cases, down the tiled hall, to the main office. Once there, we were searched, questioned, and then, when no evidence was found, released to our respective classes. Corker was fuming, but there was nothing he could do. The two of us emerged from the office, our heads held high. From that day forth we were dubbed "the gym class heroes." That was the first and last time we smoked at school.

into the woods

A warm evening breeze blew us toward the outskirts of Waverly. A guy named Evan Saddler was hosting a shindig, the likes of which wouldn't be matched for years. Even at that point, my parents had me on close watch. As far as they knew, I was crashing at the Scatterfield pad. This was partially true. We had begun our evening at Scatterfield Ranch, rallied the crew, and then headed north in the Scatterfields' blue Coupe DeVille, up the county road toward Saddler's place. Only on rare occasions, did Ben and Kathy let the boys borrow the Caddy.

The fresh air whipped in our faces, awakening dormant senses and calling us to adventure. I sunk down into the crushed blue velvet seat. The soothing sounds of Rob Zombie washed back to us from the sound system. A few people attempted to converse loudly over the music. I sat back and breathed deep hints of the approaching night.

Nick was still dating Hope at the time, who sat between he and I. Her long red hair whipped at our faces, as I fought to meet the leafy green gaze of Queen Corn, who protected us from Waverly's watchful eyes.

Red turned off the paved county road, into a small field of cars and nosed the Caddy into a vacant space. We piled out and began hoisting party supplies from the open trunk: coolers of bottles and cans, grocery bags of many many munchies, chairs, tents, flashlights, lanterns, and insect repellent.

A bonfire already roared in the evening light of the backyard, behind the unassuming white farmhouse. A tire swing hung suspended from an old oak, its invisible rider pushed along by the gentle breeze. We walked toward a small group which encircled a collapsible table in the fresh-cut grass, some distance away from the blaze. Drinks found their way into our waiting hands. Mystery punch met my tongue, a bit tart, a hint sweet.

Saddler's older sister Nikki took it upon herself to give us a tour of the grounds. Red wandered off, since he had been onsite the previous day, chain-sawing logs and clearing brush in preparation for the party. He needed no tour.

Nikki gestured toward a keg and another punchbowl near the main fire pit. She then led us down a trail toward the back of the property. The well-groomed trail was lit with torches, and zig-zagged around sizable trees and clumps of shrubs, which obscured us from the road.

We entered the first in a series of small clearings. Apostles of the herb, about twelve in total, stood passing a tightly-wrapped joint around. Puff - puff - pass, went their rhythm, puff - puff - pass, in unspoken accord. Their laughter stretched itself out across the hazy air, tickling tiny hairs on our necks, and in our ears. A few of the smokers nodded, acknowledging us.

Another cluster was off to the side shot-gunning beers. With pocket knives, they stabbed slits in the aluminum cans, twisted to open a hole, popped the top, and sucked down the barley water. Stab, twist, pop, drink. Stab, twist, pop, drink. Head rush. Alcohol flowed quickly, into subterranean bloodstreams. I spotted Zane, an acquaintance of mine. He was standing near his older brother Jared, among the shot-gunning group. I watched as they kissed the condensated aluminum cans in the shimmering shadows. Zane's dark hair was trimmed into a flat-top cut which outlined his pale features sharply. The two were laughing at some private joke.

A small greenish tent stood at one side of the clearing. Next to it, a pit had been dug into the earth. A bright blue tarp served as a liner, then ice, then case upon case of cheap beer emptied into the pit. Nikki nodded in the direction of the pit.

"That's one of two beer pits we dug out here. If Waverly's finest pay us a visit, we slide the tents over the pits."

A few bottles of colorful hard liquor dotted the pits of mass-produced generic and watery beer. I noticed a few bottles of Pucker, Jim Beam, and Jose Cuervo. Their enticing labels peeked out in the crowded pit of icy cans, as would several colorful personalities I met that night. From what holy hell did this aluminum sea arise? Sucked from the bowels of the earth to contain the seeds of our consumption...to become the litter of tomorrow's sunrise...Too much Jay, too much...

"We have lookouts posted in treestands along the road," she noted, gesturing toward the south.

In the heart of Waverly, the small-town cop shop shift-changed, debriefed, and stepped out for patrol, hoping to God for anything outside of the mind-numbing ordinary beat. Meanwhile, back at Saddler's, music manifested from a stereo somewhere in the dark. An upperclassman slapped a cold brew in Nikki's empty hand. I took in the scene. Must be over a hundred heads here, I thought.

A kid in a red and white letter jacket handed me a glowing orange-tipped joint. I took a long slow drag from the teastick and, using my thumb and index finger, passed it to a long-haired guy to my left. With that smoking pen, I signed myself into the circle. Members of our entourage trickled away in all directions to explore.

Some wandered down a path that split off to the north, toward a stand of wooded land. Others migrated to the tarp-lined beer pits, while still others headed back toward the punchbowl concoction and main bonfire.

Headlight beams continuously swept across the field where we had parked. A young couple came up the path with a bunch of canvas camp chairs. We set these up and seated ourselves. A smaller campfire was started at the center of the teahead circle. I sat my beer bottle down on a log, and pulled out Blue Magic. I produced a rolled sandwich baggie from my denim pocket, and packed the pipe with crumbled, yet sticky furry green kush. I offered the pipe to the guy at my right. Red Scatterfield's freckled face joined the circle, beer in hand.

A few hours passed in this way. Familiar and unfamiliar faces floated in and out of circles. The party churned and circulated around us, taking on a life of its own. I wandered from one half-lit circle to the next, hearing story after story, meeting person after person. The calls of night birds and crickets sang in the dark. Far off, an owl hooted her annoyance with our interruptions into her quiet night hunt.

Someone groaned when they caught the names of a few uninvited guests - a few pompous football types I had not yet met. A handful of footballers were friends of mine, but they were of the down-to-earth variety. Murmurs wafted. The words "asshole" and "prick" floated up to me. When I finally caught sight of them, I shrugged them off. Stocky, cocky fools, a dime a dozen. Brawn over brains. Were they even worth the energy of a second glance? They wandered past our smoke circle, down another trail. I took another toke when the pipe came back around, resparking the dying ember in my palm.

Not long after, I heard raised voices from the direction our uninvited guests had taken. Features on faces in our circle perked up, sensing the tension in the floating tones. Our cohort simultaneously dissolved and filtered down the trail. All went to see what the fuss was about. At the edge of the next clearing, I had to crane my neck over other onlookers to see. A kid in a hoodie blocked my view. He shifted, and then I saw two figures standing near one of the beer pits, throwing heated words at each other's way.

"If you motherfuckers think you can just come up in this party and jack our beer, you got another thing coming!" Zane's brother Jared was saying to one of the pricks that had recently arrived.

I didn't really know Jared at the time, but I liked him already. While he clearly had a home haircut, modest size, and thick glasses, I could tell he was a good dude. I looked around for his little brother, but saw no sign of him. The A-number-one asshole of the uninvited, a senior lineman named Conrad, faced Jared, holding two garbage bags of beer he had taken from the pit.

"Who the fuck are you?" Conrad snapped, dropping the bags of cans as more faces wandered up out of the dark.

"I'm one of the kids who purchased the beer you're stealing from that pit, cocksucker," he shot back, pushing his glasses up on his nose.

"Listen, trailer trash..." Conrad started.

Jared lunged at him, cracking him across the jaw. Conrad stumbled to one side, shook it off, then came back, full force, knocking Jared to the ground. Conrad was clearly used to being hit. He crouched and slammed his fist into

Jared's face, eliciting a moan.

Jared rolled away, and got back to his feet, a bit drunk and disoriented. He steadied himself, and then spat on Conrad. Jared swung and Conrad dodged, knocking Jared to the ground once more. Red Scatterfield was at my side. I felt him start to push forward in the crowd, poised to lunge. I grabbed the back of his shirt.

"No, Red. If you jump in, it'll be fucking mayhem. Right now it's one-on-one."

"But Jared's drunk, man. This kid is going to stomp the shit out of him!"

By now, the fists of the two were flying back and forth. The more Jared tried to keep himself up, the more he hit the ground. Red was straining forward, barely able to contain himself. Thankfully, Nikki ran up out of the crowd before Red pulled free of my hold.

"What the fuck, Conrad?" She huffed. "You need to get off my property right now."

Conrad stopped, fist raised, looking between her stern features and Jared slowly pulling himself up from the dirt.

"Take one beer each, and hit the road, otherwise that fucking Mustang is getting towed off my property."

Conrad thought about it for a moment, and then waved for his lackeys to follow him down the trail. The crowd parted to let them through. Several people bumping shoulders with them as they left. Red went over, grabbed an ice cold beer, and offered it to Jared, who was cleaning his cracked glasses and dusting himself off. Jared gratefully accepted the beer, taking a few sips and then holding it to his left temple.

"That took a lot of balls," Red said, seating himself beside Jared, who was now seated on a log.

Jared shrugged.

"I don't know, man. That's just bullshit."

It seemed like Red had the situation under control, so I wandered off to find Nick. The party kicked back up, us partygoers resuming the roles we had come to play. Someone offered me a fifth of Beam, which I gladly accepted. I took a few long swigs and passed it off. I found Hope and Nick down at the larger fire. I clapped Nick in a bear-hug, happy as hell to see the guy, my spirits lifted by the few minutes of his absence. We chatted for a while as the roaring fire warmed our frames.

Not long after, the first cry of, "COPS!" floated across the party. Everyone cut and ran. Some up the path to the north, into the woods. Others cut out across a cornfield toward town. Some slid into the house. Nikki stayed behind with a few close friends, executing the plan. Tents slid over pits. Miscellaneous litter found its way into big blue trash cans along the trail.

I ran like hell, joining the group that was headed northeast toward the shelter of the forest. Before long, I was at the head of a small pack that was filtering into the woods. With progressively less and less moonlight, we snaked our way among the trees and brush. Drunk and high, I grew overconfident of my night vision. I rushed on forward, blazing a trail.

At some point I took a large step out into the darkness, only to find nothing beneath my feet. I felt myself falling. About ten feet down, I hit some leaves and began to slide, knocking my knee against a rusty old washing machine that someone had dumped in the ravine.

"Fuck!" I cursed up into the darkness.

"Don't go that way." I heard a girl's voice giggle behind me.

The others changed direction and headed further along the top of the leaf-laiden rise. Clawing at loose soil and wet leaves, I crawled back up out of the ravine. Instead of running on though, I decided to lay low and listen. I smelled the forest around me, hugging me close and keeping me safe.

Were Waverly's finest really going to run up into the woods? I thought the likelihood was slim, but considered it best to be cautious. I stood, swaying on the edge of a field in the moonlight and listened for a bit. I heard no harsh or heavy tones. How long had I been gone? How far back did this forest go? I had no idea. Swallowed up by the trees were the rest of the folks in my small pack.

I crept further along the edge of the woods, thistles and thorns catching and grabbing at my pants. I saw several pairs of headlights turn out of Saddler's lot. I hung back for a minute, starting to make my way quietly across a spent cornfield in the dark. When I reached the edge of their lot, I listened again. Coast was clear.

I stumbled out of the darkness, back into one of the clearings. A few girls and a few guys looked up as I came toward them, then relaxed again, seeing I was no threat. I grabbed a beer from the reopened pit and stood near a small cluster, who were rehashing recent events. When the time came, I told my tale of the ravine and got a few laughs. Music started up again. Someone produced a dog-legged joint.

Less than half of those who ran off into the dimly-lit woods or fields returned. As smoke filtered from my lips up toward the stars, I wondered about the missing party-goers. The pole star winked down at us, brilliantly.

To this day, I like to picture my comrades, still wandering among the trees. We were running off into the uncertainty of our youth. Some would never make it. Some, like myself, returned a bit shaken and scarred, but with a bit of hard-won wisdom.

That night, the cops showed again, with an equally devastating impact on the number of partiers present. At any rate, my crew and I made it through the night, and awoke the next morning to breakfast with the remnant.

I was nursing a bit of a hangover, as well as a sore knee from my fall into the ravine, but felt better with some sausage, pancakes and maple syrup in my stomach. The remnant laughed and recounted tales of our adventures from the night before. Nick was lamenting the loss of American Woman, which had somehow gotten smashed on the rocks when the cops had come. We had a moment of silence for her.

Jared was there, and looked a little worse for the wear, his left eyebrow swollen. He didn't even remember the fight. Maybe that was a blessing. Nikki came into the room.

"Jay, your mom called. She's coming over to pick you up."

Damn, I thought. She found out I wasn't at Scatterfield's. She had probably called out there and Kathy had given her the number for Saddler's.

It was a silent ride home with my mom, silent as the grave. Such a contrast to the unfettered joy and adventure of the night before. I was grounded for several months after that escapade, but still riding high.

Ah, fuck it, I thought. It was worth it. I never again attended another party like Saddler's. We would talk about it for years to come. We definitely milked the night for all it was worth. From then on, our friend group played it safe, sticking to smaller group gatherings.

sugarcoated satellites

When we should have been in the thrall of Waverly's indoctrination, the sun clawed itself up over the trees, inviting Nick and I on yet another quest. We pulled into a parking space at Waverly High, deciding what our destination should be. We had a pocketfull of cubes, coated in Lucy, a widely-touted psychedelic substance if ever there was one.

In the front seat of his silver Chrysler, we weighed the relative merit of various locales. The echo of the tardy bell rang across the parking lot. Nick looked at me with his trademark goofy grin.

"Let's go to my cousin's townhouse, down on the west side of Mount Comfort."

"Let's roll," I confirmed.

With the destination set, the cubes hit our tongues and began to dissolve. We wove our way between the newly lined sports fields, and back out of Waverly's lot. We turned down a country road, and sped off into the morning. Windows down, we felt the rush of fresh air pound our skin as a sweet chemical sensation spread out across our tongues. We drove west, until we reached the state highway. We turned south out of Waverly. At sixty miles an hour, the cornfields flew past, giving way to rolling forest ravines and creeks. Why sit in a building for seven hours when there was all this world to see? All this adrenaline to feel? She called to us, and we very much heeded her request. County roads flew by, interspersed with the occasional entrance to a subdivision, tucked away in the woods. At some point, Nick slowed and turned left, into a collection of two-story townhomes, set back from the road.

The Chrysler swerved around a bright orange cone, marking a pothole in the lot. Nick came up alongside it, and then snatched it up. Nick would have done such a thing even stone cold sober, but I knew he was beginning to feel the effects of the cubes. My extremities were starting to tingle with anticipation as well. The roller coaster car was cranking up the first hill, preparing to drop us into the first leg of our trip. We found a parking spot, and stepped out from the car. Nick had by this point repurposed the parking cone as a megaphone. He marched across the lot, one arm swinging, one hand holding the bright orange safety cone to his lips.

"All aboard!" He called to the tops of the cars in the lot, and the empty townhome windows. "All aboooard! Train leaves the station in six minutes!"

My eyes scanned the lot, but only echoes reverberated there. Our shadows crept along behind us. They weren't going to miss out on this ride. A squirrel jabbered at us from the branch of a papery-barked birch nearby.

"Pipe down!" Nick called.

The squirrel stopped. Nick found the right townhouse, and jabbed the transparent button of her doorbell. Behind this mad conductor, I marched along for the ride. Nick's cousin Stacy sleepily opened the door. Nick again raised the cone to his lips.

"All aboooaard!" He called out to her groggy face.

Her eyes grew large, and she snatched him inside. I chuckled to myself.

"What the hell are you doing?" she asked, as she walked over to a counter and started a coffee pot to brewing.

"We are down for a trip, we are up for a trip. We have come to visit your land!"

She laughed good-naturedly, her eyes meeting mine, then Nick's.

"What are you guys on?"

Nick began to march around the room, in circles around her couch.

"The cubes, the cubes, the sugary dugary cubes," he sang out to her.

Out the patio door, the green leaves of the trees waved their farewell. I nodded to them, thanking them for seeing us off. I could sense that this was going to be one hell of a ride.

For most of the morning, I did nothing but drink orange juice and laugh. Nick shape-shifted, from conductor to court jester. He gave great speeches to the walls, the shadows, and the trees. At many times I wondered if he saw Stacy and I at all. Then, abruptly, his mind would switch tracks, veering swiftly onto something new. He was riding the stream of consciousness. On the grey couch I sat, though it felt as if I were in the stands at a magic show.

At one point, Nick caught sight of a Fisher Price kitchen, tucked under the stairs. I was watching the thoughts pour into his brain from a fluorescent kettle nearby. He tugged out the child's play kitchen, then proceeded to do the most incredible thing. He ducked down, and slipped the colorful plastic kitchen over his head. When he stood up, he wore the thing like a jacket. The kitchen swung awkwardly, as he paced to and fro, following each thought. His thoughts battled and tripped and fought to get the attention of the jester.

From my vantage point, the toy kitchen looked light as a feather, or light as a scarf. It was clear that Nick was beyond sensing its weight. For a time, he morphed into this walking talking miniature kitchen, which told strange kitchen tales. The sheer mind-melting absurdity was joy enough for me. How does the spoon feel when she gets used more often than the fork? I'm sure Nick told us, as he went about this strange scene.

At some point, the mad Lucy train made its way upstairs, as if it were ascending yet another steep drop. The train didn't travel past the first room, inside which a placid, vertical lake, spread from floor to ceiling. In the murky darkness, two strange humanlike creatures stared back at us, peering out from the reflective surface of this walled-in pond. I prodded the surface with my index finger. Ripples spread in all directions. Nick lit a cigarette. I reached over and closed the door to the small room. We were now in relative darkness. He began to weave his arm to and fro, as if conducting an orchestra with a smoking orange wand, or weaving an invisible cloak with a steaming needle.

Fireflies appeared, darting first in one direction, then another, over strangely pliant waters. Orange fireworks popped and crackled above the magical lake, while the fish faces below the surface smiled stupidly out at the show. Small orange dragons began to hiss through the air. Our minds reeled at the sight, flailing backward into space.

Our weightless forms sailed above tangerine stars, which exploded in concentric showers of light. I searched for the Milky Way, but she was nowhere to be seen. Perhaps we had frightened her, or floated too far out...I hoped she would show her face.

"Check the door of the ship!" Nick exclaimed.

I felt around where I was sure a door had been, but by that time it had melted into the infinite space on all sides.

"There's no longer any ship! Where have you taken us Nick? What have you done?"

Nick giggled like a child, as we sailed further on. We floated on bubbles in the vastness of space, a darkness dotted with the Promethean torches.

Then, as quickly as we'd lifted off, we came back down, landing on the earth with a thud. There sat a world of drywall and doors and vanity mirrors and floors. A light switch appeared, as did tile under our feet. How long did we sail? What happened to time?

"Thirty minutes until the Waverly release bell." Nick said, looking at his watch.

We opened the half-bath door, and trotted down the plush grey carpet of Stacy's stairs. Where's Stacy? I wondered, as we walked back through the living space, and then out the front door. All the toys had made it back to their respective nooks. I confusedly attempted to piece together this circle of reality to which we returned. We crossed the lot, and made it back to the car. The breeze was a soft caress upon my cheeks and the back of my neck.

As we buckled in, and turned north in Nick's silver Chrysler, I marveled at the difference a day or an hour can make in one's life. The sun filtered through the trees and sparkled off creeks as we drove on in silence. As we headed on closer to Waverly High, I pictured the rows of desks in the classroom, eyes on the board, hands taking notes. I knew I didn't have all the answers, but intuited that it wasn't for me. I was lusting for life, and was not about to let Waverly stand in my way.

the pinehouse grille

As soon as I was able, I marched up into the Waverly High guidance department and procured a work permit for myself. I was itching to start making my own cash and not be so leashed to my parents. It was damn humiliating having to beg them for cash at every turn, cash which was often held over my head as an enticement to behave appropriately. Even when I did chores, it wasn't like I was well-compensated.

I had some friends and acquaintances at the local Pinehouse Grille, a one-story brick building with a low, sloping roof just off the interstate. A giant billboard behind the restaurant shot up toward the grey sky, enticing road-weary travelers off the asphalt for some down-home pot roast and mashed potatoes smothered in gravy.

I put in my application there and got a call the same day. When I arrived for my interview, a short and bubbly cashier named Chelsey walked me through the restaurant to a plastic leather booth. I shook hands with a short, wavy-haired guy named Terry, the hiring manager. I can't remember what the starting pay was, but it wasn't much. Maybe as low as $5.75/hr. I wasn't too worried though, since I'd be working a chill spot with normal human beings. There was plenty of opportunity to move up in the ranks. I heard from friends that raises happened regularly. I went out and purchased some work clothes from a local Wal-Mart: tan Dickies, pants that were so thick and rough it felt like being wrapped in canvas. At any rate, they were cheap and durable.

I started as a dishwasher, the worst possible position in the place. That was where most males started. Most females started as cashier or hostess, or possibly buffet. The busboys brought back huge brown busbins piled high with dirty dishes and half-eaten food. For entire shifts, the mounds of filth flowed back to me. I sprayed each dish off with the giant spray head, battling filth with a high-pressure wash. I sorted them into corresponding stacks, and then slung them into the pale blue hard plastic dish racks. I then shoved them through the industrial washer/sanitizer. Spray, stack, sling, push. Spray, spray, stack, sling, push...for hours upon hours upon hours.

I wore a thick green vinyl apron, which prevented my navy Pinehouse Grille shirt from getting soaked. The water from the spray nozzle ran off the apron, down onto my leather shoes, which soaked up the dirty water. It was fucking gross - utterly terrible, but I had to start somewhere. I came home smelling like I had crawled out of a dumpster, squishing in those nasty-ass leather shoes. At night I dreamt rivers of dirty dishes, caked with mac and cheese and chicken pot pie. What unholy hell? But I knew it wouldn't last forever. I had my eye on the grill, and soon enough I began training to grill steaks and run the fryers. Hard work began to pay off.

Jared happened to be one of the few and the proud veterans at Pinehouse Grille. As you've seen, I ran into Jared a few times prior to working at the Grille, but really got to know him there. He was a pimple-faced kid, with a standard campy haircut, and wore thick glasses. You'd think he was a colossal nerd if you didn't know any better. He came from a poor family in Waverly, and lived in a rundown three bedroom house with his mom, his brother Zane, and his little sister Mandy. Shortly after we met, his mom's boyfriend Jason moved in. Jason was a heavy metal guitarist with sleeves of tribal tattoos and straight brown hair which extended down to his knees.

Jared was the hardest worker in his whole damn family. Unlike his mom, who hopped from low-paying job to low-paying job, Jared worked long shifts at the Grille. His girl Crystal did the same. She was a sweet, mild-mannered cashier with straight, sand-colored hair.

In his free time, Jared loved on Crystal and wrenched on cars. He was always pulling an engine out of this car, changing the brakes on that... Jared and Crystal were dead set on escaping Waverly. At the very least, they had their sights set on a nice house in Mount Comfort, just out of Waverly's reach. Jared worked, and scraped and saved. That being said, he wasn't any straight-laced tight-ass. He knew how to get down. Metalhead Jason would buy ale and spirits for us if we expressed our intention to stay on the premises. So, many weekends were spent moderately intoxicated at that rundown house, with the dirty-blue vinyl siding, in the heart of Waverly.

At Jared's birthday bash one year, someone bought him a blow-up sheep as a joke. After we'd downed enough Honey Browns and whiskey, we could be seen running through the streets of Waverly, kicking rocks and shouting "she-eeeeep, sha-eeeep" at the top of our lungs, as if we were out in search of a lost member of the flock.

One day, I was working the afternoon shift at the Pinehouse, when someone shouted that Jared was out back, acting a fool. I squared away the grill, and then headed back to see what the fuss was about. Nick had pulled up at the service entrance and Jared lay sprawled in the back seat, babbling like an idiot. They'd come from his little brother Zane's birthday shindig at their dad's house.

Their dad was an alcoholic who lived in a little village north of Waverly, a village whose only claim to fame was that John Dillinger had once robbed the bank there. Their dad lived around the corner from that infamous bank, and if you got him drunk or stoned enough would pick up the guitar and break into some godawful song about a bear which he had written decades earlier, in his hayday. The guy really was one sad son-of-a-bitch.

Now, Jared didn't smoke, but he could drink like a fish. He came by it honestly... Generational baby steps, I guess. That night, he had so much to drink that the bastard couldn't conquer gravity enough to sit up. As one of us held the restaurant's back door open, manager Rob peered into the backseat through the open window of Nick's Crysler. Rob was slightly overweight, with a crew cut and several bad teeth. He reminded me of a fat pirate, or a Navy reject. He smirked down at Jared.

"Hey Jared, you look like you could use a shower!"

With that, Rob reached over and grabbed a sprayer which was attached to the nearby janitorial sink. Streams of water hit Jared in the face, which prompted him to howl up at the crescent moon, while the majority of the staff looked on, laughing. Jared shielded his face with his arms and cursed at Nick to hit the gas. Nick threw up a peace sign, shoved the car into gear and they whirled off into the night, Jared howling as they disappeared.

Tre Moreno also walked into my life at the Grille. Moreno's dad wasn't really in the picture at that point. He lived with his Spanish-speaking mother and little brother in a modest beige house. They were tucked-away on one of Waverly's many pot-holed streets. When I first saw the house, it appeared as if the giant pines were attempting to shove the house off the lot, so overgrown and expansive were they.

Tre usually had his long black hair pulled back out of his face while at Pinehouse, though he let it fall across his face in school. Moreno was stocky, and dressed in skater clothes when not at the Grille. Tre worked buffet, like Jared, and was known for his hilarious, dry sense of humor. Tre smoked about as much weed as I did in those days, though he was known to chase it with a Xanax pill or two at times. He could be seen shuffling to and from the buffet, singing Jim Morrison tunes, as he flung spent pans of apple crisp into the dish-washing area:

"I'll tell you a story of hippies, and misfits, and zen, da-duh-da..."

You could always tell Tre's mood by whether he was humming or singing. And if he was singing, what was his tone and inflection?

One day a mousy new girl started at Pinehouse, and for whatever reason, Moreno was assigned to train the poor girl. Rob should have known better. All went well for most of the morning, until it came time to clean up the Saturday buffet, switching it over from brunch to lunch and dinner cuisine. The girl asked Tre what she should do with the waffle iron. Tre, with a completely straight face, instructed:

"Now this here waffle iron is kind of unique. It's older, so it's a bit quirky.

The best way to cool this thing down, after you unplug it, is for you to take those oven mitts there and carefully set it on the ground. After you've done that, you gotta stand on the thing for about five minutes, until it feels cool to the touch."

The girl's trusting green eyes looked up at Moreno seriously. She nodded her head, trying hard to remember the instructions: Unplug, use oven mitts, set on ground, stand on it. Once the girl had done as Tre instructed, he told her to set her watch for a full five minutes. He then calmly walked around the corner, and ran back to find me at the grill. He was laughing so hard, he could barely get the words out.

"Go scope out that new girl up in buffet," he thumbed toward the front of the store, laughing so hard that tears had begun to form.

I headed toward the buffet, down the brown tiled hall, and peeked around the corner. There the girl stood, two white shoes close together on top of the cast-iron waffle maker. She gazed off into space, patiently waiting for five minutes to be up. I raced back to Moreno, who was still heaving with laughter back in the grill area. By that time, I was cracking up too.

"You're such a fucker," I gasped between laughs. "What the hell is she thinking?"

Tears rolled down Tre's cheeks.

"She's waffling!" He giggled.

With great effort, I pulled myself together, and went into Rob's office.

"Rob, you gotta go check out that new girl up at the buffet. She's acting kind of strange."

Rob swung around in his swivel chair, away from the computer. He stood up and marched out to the buffet. When he spotted the new girl, a confused look came over his features. He stared at her shoes on the waffle iron, hands on hips, an eyebrow raised.

"Whatcha doing, hun?"

The new girl got this deer-in-the headlights look.

"I'm... cooling down the waffle iron," she told Rob, innocently.

"What? Oh, no, sweetie," Rob said, correcting her. "You can just put these things away. You don't have to stand on them first."

Her cheeks flushed, and she stepped down onto the tile floor. Rob went back and slapped Tre upside the back of his head. Needless to say, that girl didn't last too long at the Grille.

Other times, Tre would have me send unsuspecting employees to the walk-in freezer, for a box of this, or a box of that. He would be lying in wait, and pelt them with clusters of frozen corn kernels or mixed veggies once the door had closed on them. They would turn and sprint back through the door under heavy fire, cursing as they went.

One time, I made the mistake of stopping into work to pick up my check after I had dropped some Lucy. By my pupil size, and my changed demeanor, Moreno sensed it right away. He hopped around the corner, and came at me, waddling and opening and shutting an umbrella which he had picked up from

God-knows-where. Squawking, he chased me round and round the back of the restaurant, until I was able to escape out the back. He cackled and made strange faces at me. I was convinced Bruce Wayne's archnemesis, the Penguin was out to get me.

When I wasn't holed up in my basement room grounded, or hanging at the Scatterfield Ranch, or bumming around Waverly's country roads, I was at the Pinehouse, working hard and having a grand old time. After the Grille had closed for the night, we often hopped in each others' cars to drink or smoke or just shoot the shit. It wasn't a bad way to get out of the house and get some kicks.

the teacher's edition

One of my "side hustles" at Waverly High was flipping teacher's edition textbooks. The effort was born out of a desire to avoid Waverly High's assembly line, where useless and irrelevant information was to be packed, undigested, into our young minds. Back in those days, a vast majority of the teachers taught straight out of one textbook or another, lording the language over us in a godlike way. We quickly saw through the web of distraction Waverly had woven for us.

As I sat in Mr. Fish's Algebra II class, bored out of my skull, my eyes lit upon the teacher's edition of the textbook we were using for that class. It was peeking out from underneath a paper-clipped stack of homework papers. When the bell rang, signaling the end of the class period, I snagged that book in the hustle and bustle of kids coming and going, the teacher engrossed in conversation with class pets. I used that original teacher's edition myself, but it occurred to me how valuable such a book was to those who wanted to play the game as efficiently as possible.

I began to snag other teacher's edition books, even for classes in which I was not enrolled. The books brought around $50-70 a pop. Some people wanted to haggle over the cost, which was fine by me. It was all profit anyway. Once people had their hands on T.E. books, I recommended that they then give or sell answer sheets to others in the class to help buy some loyalty and make their money back. When I told my guy Nick Scatterfield about my little scheme, he just grinned and shook his head saying,

"I think God gave your gifts to the wrong guy."

"Haha, Nick. That's where you're wrong. God didn't design us to march around in a robotic haze."

You would think that teachers would go off script, with all their teacher's editions disappearing, but most of them just kept on trucking. Old habits die hard.

I was dating a freshman named Madeline at the time. She had crimped brown hair, and a flare for trouble. You could tell she was "no good" from the way she raised one eyebrow and smirked. She was not one of those girls who needed a sandwich, and I liked that. I didn't want a girl who would blow away if a good wind came along. Soon after we began dating, we arranged for her to get a ride to the end of my parents' long gravel drive. I helped her climb through my open window, passing her a stool and holding her hand as she stepped up and over the pine ledge. She smelled like the night, and like sweet pea body spray. We kissed a few times and then went over and climbed beneath my comforter. Maddie shyly undressed and we had "safe sex" in the comfort of my blacklit basement bedroom to the melancholy vocals of the Moody Blues. That was her first time, and my second. My mom almost walked in and discovered us, but luckily I had the wherewithal to roll into a position where her body was obscured and I looked to be asleep. Another close call.

Maddie started assisting me in the T.E. scheme. It was becoming easier to grab-and-go with one person distracting the teacher, and the other making the grab. We had to be careful, since word was starting to get around, but at the height of this endeavor, we had it down to a science. I would distract, while she snagged the book.

This whole racket was going pretty smoothly, and we were actually making a good amount of cash. We were passing all our classes with flying colors, as was almost everyone else in the classes we hit. But I knew, as well as anyone that we couldn't keep this up indefinitely. Waverly would attempt to outflank us at some point. I just wanted to push the limits and see how far we got. To me, everything was like some grand experiment, tampering with the systems in place to test and determine the boundaries.

Maddie and I were growing ever closer, feeling ourselves a little too strong. We continued our scheme at school and tried new things when alone. Riding that tide of hormones, we admittedly had grown to feel a bit invincible. Things peaked when I borrowed my dad's SUV and we drove out to the WWII museum parking lot to watch the 4th of July fireworks. Out in that empty parking lot, we put down the tailgate of the SUV, rolled out sleeping bags and pillows. We started kissing and heavy petting, and made love to the bursting fireworks overhead and Pink Floyd's Division Bell echoing through the speakers as our soundtrack. When we had finished, I disposed of the condom and we cleaned up. We lay on our backs talking of the future and watching the colorful tendrils of explosions in the sky overhead.

When our side hustle did come crashing down, it was in quite an extreme and unexpected manner. Maddie was spotted in the act, as she bagged a T.E. book in a geometry classroom. I was acting as the distraction. A teacher's pet named Toby noticed Maddie making the grab out of the corner of his eye. Toby, as we soon found out, was definitively in Waverly's pocket. This was his opportunity to gain even more respect and admiration from the teacher. He waited until Madeline and I were gone, and then he shot up out of his seat, as if driven by an engine. That invisible engine propelled him over to the teacher's desk, where he promptly informed the teacher of what had transpired.

I was in Woody's shop class when I got the news that Maddie had been expelled. Word travels amazingly fast when there are eyes and ears on the ground. I didn't have a short fuse, but I did have a fuse nonetheless. I had shop class last period, and it was my favorite class, so I finished planing down the top for a table I was making, and then peaced out.

I called Maddie later that evening when I got home. She was hanging out on the back patio smoking some homegrown. She wasn't angry, just seemed surprisingly resigned to her fate.

"It was only a matter of time, Jay. I'm kinda glad to have the weight of school off my shoulders."

I was confused. I hadn't expected her to concede victory to Waverly so easily. She knew who had ratted her out - Tobias Templeton. Admin pegged her as the mastermind behind the whole teacher's edition scandal. She had already been written up for several other petty offenses that year, so he was done - out for the year. Madeline was asked by the administration if there were any accomplices, but she hadn't cracked.

That night, as I sat listening to DMX, a popular and obnoxious rap artist in those years, the situation churned over and over in my head. I simmered as I wrestled with this latest win for Waverly. She caught me off guard. I was lulled into a false sense of security. I hadn't reckoned the racket would end like this. I guess I thought that a few of us might get a slap on the wrist from Gordo, but I never thought anyone would get expelled over it. I never foresaw that futures would be altered. What's that commonly cited adage? Pride comes before the fall? Yep. Pride. I had plenty of it. And not the good kind. The impulsive, overconfident kind. The more I rolled the situation over, the more I paced my room, fists clenched, as the music chided me on. I was still naive enough to believe I could fight fate.

Thoughts began to rain down on me faster than I could compute: This snob Toby would float through his high school years, above any nonsense. Madeline wouldn't even be a blip on his radar in a few weeks. He couldn't see clearly that he was working with a corrupt system. He wouldn't even realize that his snitchery had cost a good kid her diploma - her ticket out of a failing town. Maddie was a good kid after all. She just had the tendency to get sucked into the sketchy situations around her. Looking back on my twisted teenage logic, I think that I somehow sensed that Toby represented something larger, something more systematic, something I despised - whole generations of yesmen, flowing in an out of the schools, in and out of white collar jobs, while those who questioned Waverly and what she was feeding us got stepped on like bugs by the system.

I fell asleep that night fuming in the darkness, ceaselessly agitated. I awoke with a silent rage tucked inside my chest. Something had to be done about Toby. I would confront him myself.

I skipped the morning smoke that next day, showered, and got ready for school. I asked my father to drop me off early for school. I told him I had a test to make up. My dad looked at me suspiciously, surprised by my sudden burst of proactivity. But he agreed to drop me off on his way to work. I got jacked up on the soundwaves of several metal bands I listened to in those days, their angry screams flowing into my ears and fuelling the fire. Meshuggah, Rammstein, Static X, and others. As I stepped out of his SUV, my dad wished me a good day and sped off to another world.

I shuffled slowly across the concrete apron which skirted the northside of the school. Several small maple trees stood glistening in the morning sun, boxed in by concrete on all sides. What a shame they would never grow to their full potential... With fists tucked deep inside my Jnco pockets, I ran through scenarios and weighed the consequences of what I planned to do. I tugged at the large steel handle of Waverly's door. She welcomed me into the unusually quiet halls. Here and there a voice echoed off the half cinder block, half wallpapered walls. A janitor was buffing a floor near the gym. I strolled down the wide main corridor of the school, and instead of entering the cafeteria, hung a sharp right, past the boys' restroom. I hooked a left down a smaller hall and found Red Scatterfield near his locker, toward the southwest side of the school.

"I'm confronting that Toby kid, Red. Know where he's at?" I asked.

I had no idea what the kid looked like. He was a grade beneath me, and while I had probably seen him in passing, we didn't run in the same circles. He had been invisible to me, off my radar.

"Alright, Jay," Red said, raising an eyebrow, "Let's go for a walk."

We made our way back through the main corridor of the school, the way I had come. We hung a left into the hallway which ran parallel to the northside of the school, near the double doors that had welcomed me minutes earlier. Adrenaline drove us onward. Our shoulders squared, chests stuck out like apes out for tribal control. When we had made it a quarter of the way down the hallway, Red pointed Toby out to me.

"There he is, bro. The tall kid. Bright blue polo."

Toby was walking straight toward me, down the middle of the hallway, studying his Doc Martens, oblivious to the shitstorm that was coming his way. This storm was blowing in from a different universe, one Toby couldn't even fathom.

"Tobias Templeton?" I asked when we reached each other, I blocking his path.

His eyes came up to meet mine. Confusion spread across his features. He didn't know who I was, or why I was there. I shook my head, signaling my disgust and displeasure. He cocked his head and eyed me uncomprehendingly. He opened his mouth to speak, but I gripped my chrome Zippo lighter tight in my right fist. I swung. The first hit landed on his temple, a right hook before he could speak. He dropped to the floor. If I had been expecting a fight, I had clearly been mistaken. My lanky frame rained a few more punches down at him, and a few more kicks in the side for good measure. Then the storm blew over. As quickly as it had come, my anger was gone.

Several students had begun to gather. It was over so fast that most didn't even know what happened. Red was chuckling and shaking his head. We continued on toward the other end of the hallway. Over our shoulders, we heard some girl asking,

"Ummm, can you move him? I need to get to my locker."

Red and I started to crack up, breaking the tension. We headed back toward his locker, shared the story with a few people, and then headed on to our first classes of the day. After the morning announcements, Gordo's voice came over the PA:

"Jay Chapparal, please come to the main office. Jay Chapparal, to the main office. Thank you."

I was in Small Engines class at the time, rebuilding a lawn mower engine. It was noisy in there, and no one was paying attention to the overhead speaker. I ignored the request. The main principal came over the PA and repeated the request for my presence in the main office. My hand had been sliced open by the Zippo lighter, which had popped open during a punch. I washed and nursed my hand with the supplies in the Small Engines room. The end of class bell rang. Another request for my presence. This time I went down.

The principals told me that Toby had been taken to the hospital to get staples in his head. For the first time, I was speechless. Staples? Jesus. What kind of monster was I? That escalated quickly: 0 to 60. Waverly had me all messed up. I recovered my cool. The head principal asked me for my account of what went down. I told them Toby and I had gotten in a disagreement, and that this, in turn, had led to a physical altercation. They pumped me for more specifics. I knew I shouldn't say too much, but I did mention that the disagreement related to Toby getting my girlfriend expelled. Not only was this true, but it granted an aire of legitimacy to my rage. I said something to the effect that,

"I understand that issues shouldn't be resolved through physical violence, but I get very defensive about the ones I love, and Toby came for Madeline so I came for him".

The administrators listened attentively, and then stepped out to talk amongst themselves. The head principal stepped back in and gave me the verdict: 3-day suspension.

I don't remember much of what I did during those three days out of school. One day my father took me down to the local Kraft factory, where his company had an expansion project going on. I saw workers doing their repetitive tasks, machines spitting out caramel cubes and lucky charm marshmallows. I'm not sure what my father was trying to teach me, but I did walk away from the experience with some perspective. Did I want to run a marshmallow machine for the rest of my days? Emphatically the fuck not.

While suspended, there had been talk of Toby's older brother coming after me. Evidently his older brother was a lineman on the football team, and had some pretty tough friends. Red found this out and moved quickly to nip it in the bud. He assembled a group of guys and confronted Toby's brother and his crew in the parking lot, out by the old oak. Red, Nick, Jared, and others made it real clear that whatever Templeton's guys tried against me would come back at them several times over.

“Surely you guys don’t want to be kicked off the team, do you?” Red taunted, indicating with a nod of his head the back of the football scoreboard, which advertised a local car dealership.

Red’s stocky frame stood firm, his intentions not unclear. His red hair wafted in the wind. His piercings glistened in the afternoon sun. The lineman stood between Red and Waverly High, as if defending her walls from attack. Templeton’s guys were silent, attempting to stare Red and the others down.

I wouldn’t have wanted to be in their shoes. Red wasn’t their size, but he wasn’t quite “right” in the head either. In fact, he was more than a little nuts. The previous summer, he had his ring finger pulled off in an accident at the local UPS shipping center. He flashed that disfigured hand at them - the hand with the missing ring finger. Toby’s brother stared at that spot where the ring finger should have been. After a long, dramatic pause, they finally relented, turning and making their way back toward the school. Red called out to their backs,

“I recommend that you let this blow over, but you think about it and let us know.”

Red turned and looked back at all the guys who stood behind him, many of whom had reputations for being just a bit “off.” He smiled a big smile and shook up with Jared, Nick, and a few of the others before the group dispersed and went their separate ways.

That was the last we ever heard about Toby or his brother. We had suffered some casualties at Waverly’s hands, but Red held off her defenders for another day. The battle was a draw, but the dust settled on the teacher’s edition episode.

Still I couldn’t believe it. Maddie was out. I sensed that with the absence of shared experience, Waverly would begin to divide us, pull us apart. The division bell had sounded and Waverly was moving in. I could sense it. I spoke to Maddie on the phone in the evenings, until one night when she called me all jacked up on air duster. She had just huffed and her voice was deep, really deep. The boredom of Waverly’s long hours began to eat away at her. She had begun to huff ether and duster, among other substances generally available to Waverly’s teaheads and townies. With the unraveling underway, I began to call less and less, and eventually dropped off contact, feeling powerless to wrench her away from Waverly’s greedy hands.

our towering competence

Kathy, the female parental unit of the Scatterfield household raised the kitchen window and began to 'holler' down into the yard, when she spotted six or seven of us moving toward the vehicles, dressed in pitch-black from head to toe.

The Scatterfields had a walk-out basement with a sliding patio door that opened onto a concrete patio, bordered by chipped terra-cotta pots in which grew pansies, weeds and grass. Concrete steps, in which chunks of limestone had been set, guided feet to a sidewalk leading up around the southeast corner of the house. The walk then terminated at the gravel parking area and driveway, near the often-used firepit.

The open kitchen window was one of Kathy's favorite perches from which to monitor our activity. We were often to be seen around the bonfire pit in the front yard or near the pond, which was also nestled out front over a small berm. A tall pole, from which a knotted rope hung, stood near the dock.

Red was just pulling the patio door closed behind him when Kathy started up.

"Nicholas!" She screeched, seeing Nick leading the way up the limestone stairs.

I could see the silhouette of her round, curly-hair in the well-lit window. I caught a glint off her wide-framed glasses as I tromped up the walk.

"Where you guys going dressed like that? Nick! Red? Jack!" She kept squawking at the backs of her boys until Nick responded.

"We'll be careful Kathy. Be back in a bit."

I chuckled to myself as I pulled a black skullcap over my ears. I felt kinda bad for Kathy, who kept squawking at our backs in the early night. The scent of fresh-cut grass still hung in the air.

We piled into the back of Red's blue monster truck, snaked our way down the Scatterfield's long gravel drive, dust rising up and settling on the long grass. We turned west onto Rush Line Road. I clung to a chrome rollbar which was bolted into the truck bed. Each of us took in deep lungfuls of night air as we sped toward our towering destination.

Near the golf course, a few miles down the road, was a radio tower. We parked behind the bushes in an empty business parking lot, then piled out in the direction of the tower. Some lept out, while some climbed carefully down. We looked straight up into the night sky. Slivers of spotty clouds slid across the waxing moon. A beacon flashed at the apex of the tower, its flashes reflected off the running clouds. The structure was a small pyramid of criss-crossed steel with a platformed top. Two large wedge-shaped radio transmitters sat perched like sleepy metal birds atop the steel frame. They spilled their invisible waves out across the inky blanket of the night. We snuck through a stand of pines and shrubs to find ourselves beside a small flat-roofed building at the base.

"Now's the time, if anyone wants out," Red prompted, scanning faces.

We all made eye contact in the dim light. We had come this far. No one wanted to back down yet. Nick turned and began to climb. One by one we scaled the chain-link fence which butted up to the side of the small control building. From the top of the fence, each of us pulled ourselves, or were assisted, up onto the flat roof, which was covered in smooth river-rocks that shifted under the soles of our boots. The top of the control building was close enough where we could reach over and climb onto the base of the tower.

The painted red and white steel was cool and dry on our pale hands. The group spirit carried us on. Once I saw the feet of the person before me at eye level, my hands grasped the welded rungs of the ladder and began to climb. Adrenaline called to us from on high, promising a rush that was worth the climb. There were two stopping points on the lower levels of the tower, cross-hatched walkways that spanned the perimeter of the tower. A few people looked straight up the ladder which would be the final long stretch of the climb. We had already climbed 50-75 ft, and the last ladder which rose toward the sky was easily another 100 ft up, with no breaks. A few people got nervous, or maybe wise, and decided to remain on the comfortable height of the second level.

The others and I began to ascend. The climbing became hypnotic, one foot, then the next, one hand, then the next.

"Don't look down!" someone called from above.

I became one with the rhythm of the climb. One rung, then the next, one rung, then the next. Soon enough, my head popped up through an opening in the steel mesh platform. I pulled myself up through the opening, and then assisted the two that followed.

I stood upright. We could see miles in every direction. The cars were beetles below, winding up and down their asphalt paths. Nick and Red already lay on their backs staring up at the stars, which hung just out of reach. I lay down and did the same.

How much trust we have in our fellow humans, I thought, as I lay up on that steel altar beneath the heavens. I thought about the unknown hands that had assembled the structure under us. The complex wonder of it all blew my young mind. Nick had rolled onto his belly and was now hanging his head over the side of the platform. I did the same.

Adrenaline poured herself into us through every pore. Every unhindered hair on us detected the subtleties of the night wind. The adrenaline on offer allowed us to imagine ourselves strange steel-legged guardians of this alien landscape before us. Our consciousness ascended on this light-speckled night.

After a time, some sat up. Some rose to our feet.

"Have we had our fill?" Red asked, looking at us others.

"Not yet," I said impulsively, and walked over to the giant, grey wedge-shaped transmitter on the northwest corner of the platform.

The transmitter had hand and foot-holds where its steel sheets had been both riveted and soldered together. I began to climb that last 15-20 feet. My lanky body scampered up the back, a lizard on the cold steel surface. Soon my head peaked out above the transmitter. The vastness of the rolling land simultaneously amazed and humbled me. I felt a wave of gratitude at the reality of being alive, truly alive, and awake to experience this special night.

"You know you probably won't be able to have kids now," Red joked from the platform below.

I laughed and began to scale carefully back down.

"Ah, one night of radioactivity never hurt anyone," I shot back. "Besides, we've smoked so much weed that a little radiation is the least of our worries."

We were full of talk and laughter from that point on, as gravity's gentle hands guided us back down to earth. We slowly rejoined our level two friends, and then finished our descent.

That climb was not our last visit to the tower. We ascended it many more times in those days when we craved an escape from Waverly's mundanity. Are we to blame for taking such risks when they paid our souls so handsomely?

In a dry and utterly predictable land, our thirst for adventure was often quenched in such ways. Now I have my own son, and I often wonder if I would wish such experiences for him. He needs to feel the extremes of life at some point, and the safe space of a book or film can only take him so far...

rumschpringe

The girls and I were riding high, following a lazy afternoon clam-bake session. I had recently begun to twist and tease my coarse hair into dreadlocks, and I toyed with one of the dreads distractedly as we rolled along down Waverly's main drag. I sat up tall in the back seat of Sam's Grand Prix. Sam was a mellow, lanky bleach-blonde girl with a nose ring and a steady smirk. She clothed herself in Grateful Dead t-shirts and baggy corduroy. Her dad was on the school board, so I often had the pleasure of appearing before him and "the good 'ol boys," as I battled the Waverly administration. Jade's face was more full, and was framed by dark ringlets which cascaded down onto her shoulders. She was blessed with that mediterranean beauty which stems from mild climates and sun-kissed afternoons. Her laughter was infectious, piercing even the most unyielding face in her presence. I flung my hand out the back window, feeling the pulse of the sky. The three of us regularly rode through Waverly and her countryside, looking for laughter on her gravel roads.

As we pulled up to a stop light on Main Street, we turned up Marley and the Wailers, basking in the afternoon's glory. The Pinehouse Grille stood off to our right, and I eyed the building, thankful I wasn't scheduled to work that afternoon. We waited in the left turn lane, ready to proceed toward Archie's Sandwich Shop, which was often our munchie destination. As we waited our turn, Sam drummed on the steering wheel. Our heads bobbed as Bob sang "Could you be Loved." A large blue passenger van pulled up beside us. Men with long beards and black hats peered out from the windows. Each wore a solid-colored shirt and black vest or suspenders as well. A young beardless face among the group inspected us quizzically. The driver appeared to be a relatively normal cat, who wore sunglasses and a loose-fitting, button-up bahama shirt. Marley, in the background, continued to play.

"Scope out this driver," I motioned to the girls, from the backseat. "What's his deal? I thought the Amish were against any kind of modern tech?"

Sam looked over, and waved to the driver, who quickly looked away. Jade flashed a lazy, stoned smile at the group.

"I think their official stance is that technology is evil, or at least that it negatively impacts their faith."

I mulled this over for a second.

"So they are fine with riding in a van, but not driving it? That's a fucking technicality if I ever heard one! That's ludicrous! The driver can burn in hell as far as they are concerned, as long as they get their ticket to heaven? Man, fuck the Amish! Fuck - thee - Ah - mish! How selfish is that? What kind of a petty god do they think God is?"

By this point Sam and Jade were cracking up, thrown off by my sudden outburst. Sam would open up her mouth to say something, but before she could speak, I would come at her with,

"No, Sam. Fuck the Amish. Fuck - thee - Ah - mish!" This only set the two laughing all-the-harder.

The light turned green, and Sam, with tremendous effort, gripped the wheel with her long thin fingers, making the left turn, followed by an immediate right, into Archie's parking lot. She was wiping tears from her eyes with the sleeve of her dead-head shirt. Still Marley played on. She pulled into a spot on the far side of the lot. I started giggling at their laughter, and before long we were overcome with laughter, each person infecting the next. This laughter was a force which came swirling down on us. One of us would start to catch a breath, only to be sparked again by the next person. Still the Wailers sang. The wisps of passing clouds drug their late afternoon shadows smoothly across the asphalt lot, as, with much effort, we collected ourselves from within our cloud of idiocy and stepped out to slake our cotton-mouths and rumbling stomachs.

Ultimately, I couldn't care less what the Amish do or don't do. I have no open hostility toward those who see deodorant and gas-guzzling as the work of the devil....I think I was just tickled by the absurdity of their hypocritical stance toward technology...But then again, all systems have their own internal logic, which often looks absurd to outsiders. I wish them well in their endeavors, and I actually appreciate a few of their concepts…

Take rumschpringe, for instance, when they send their young out into the world to experience "the work of the devil's hands". There's a kind of wisdom to it, testing the limits of reality...And maybe, just maybe, that's what this whole Waverly High thing was ultimately all about for me…rumschpringe.

I looked up from my sandwich, coming back to our shared reality.

"Hey Sam, did you know Marley died from skin cancer?"

"Damn, why you gotta be such a buzz-kill, Jay?"

"It's just crazy to think about...all those years of smoking tea and partying, then you get taken up outta here by the sun...that's tuff…"

Another time I was hanging with the girls shit didn't go so well. We shouldn't have gone out... But we didn't have shit else to do... But we had bud and time... But spent cornfields stared out at us like some leaf-eared beige god challenging us to find the fun which it had hidden in the Indiana fields.

At that stage, our life was a fog, so when the fog rolled in that night, we welcomed the transformation she brought to our bland and monotonous existence. It was the outward manifestation of our inner space. The girls stopped by and picked me up around two in the afternoon from my parents' place, out in the rolling stretch of farmland northwest of Waverly. Sam was driving, and Jade sat shotgun in Sam's plum-colored Pontiac GrandPrix.

As we bumped on down the gravel road that was my parents' drive, I must have packed up the bowl with some fresh herbal remedies.

Our standard procedure was to pass the pipe and plumb the depths of the country roads, which stretched out their welcoming weblike hands in all directions. At any rate, we had woven our way into Waverly's vicinity on our excursion. There was always smoke, and music, and laughter, and smoke, all circulating among whoever happened to be along for the ride.

On this particular grey afternoon, the interior air of the car looked not unlike the exterior air: fog-laden.

We rounded a curve and came to a stop at an intersection on north Main Street. We laughed. We toked. Sam looked to the left to see if the intersection was clear, but as I said, it was foggy, and on top of that, her vision was obstructed by an old oak - a giant of a tree - at least four feet thick.

A Lincoln Towncar came barreling down on us, manifesting swiftly from within the belly of the fog. Halfway across the intersection, the enormous car ploughed into the side of that unfortunate Grand Prix. We heard squealing tires and breaking of glass and folding of fiberglass. We had been served up a t-bone by some unfortunate fool.

All this took place in front of a local dentist's office in Waverly, and people poured out of the waiting room to slake their concern or curiosity.

I grabbed the bowl off the floor, pocketed it, and then, thinking quick, told the girls to hand me all the paraphernalia they had. Sam and Jade quickly stuffed lighters, bags, and bowls into my outstretched hands. I told them to feed the police a story about picking up a random guy named Tim from the bowling alley.

As curious folks made their way toward the wreckage which sat incapacitated in the thick fog, I stepped out and started walking swiftly toward a shrub-lined alley. A few individuals questioned me as my footsteps picked up speed. I mumbled something to them, but didn't stop. As soon as I rounded the corner of the dentist office, I broke into a full sprint. The gravel crunched underfoot. I ran my heart out for a few blocks.

When I was certain I wasn't being followed, I stopped, taking stock of my surroundings. I deposited all paraphernalia into a nearby shrub. I studied it, noting the location and appearance down in memory. I then changed my appearance a bit and continued on at a casual walking pace for a few more blocks to the YMCA, where I phoned Nick for a ride.

The girls spoke with the police, and made it back to Sam's place uneventfully. The Grand Prix was totaled. Waverly's fog had overtaken us that day. We were shaken up, but I returned the next day to retrieve the stash. I had one more story in the bag.

jack beats the devil

As I've mentioned, being a bit of a grifter got the adrenaline rush going - the challenge of the theft. From only God knows where, I lifted a black American Eagle coat and graciously gifted it to Jack Scatterfield - the youngest of the Scatterfield Boys. Jack had matured and begun to run with our crew. At one of our late fall Friday night bonfires, Jack was wearing this puffy, down-filled coat, with the emblem of an eagle in flight on the upper right quadrant of the chest.

We were at the Scatterfield Ranch, obscured by the treeline which stood between us and the road. As Nick and I worked at building the fire, feeding dry wood into the hungry, outstretched fingers of flame, frivolities began. Some passed around a tightly-rolled joint, while others cracked a beer or tipped a bottle back. Some moved to avoid the shifting smoke.

Gradually, new faces appeared from out of the darkness, to assemble around the flaming pile of chopped wood. The gathering topped out at about fifteen people, an average size for one of our regular post-Saddler get-togethers. The group was in good spirits, and pretty mellow on this particular night. We were seated in colorful canvas camp chairs, or on large logs.

At one point, Will McClellan, an abnormally tall, goofy kid with a military-style buzz-cut, had everyone doubled over with laughter. He began to tell a story about an interviewee and a news anchor. At one point the news anchor asked her guest a question.

The response to the news anchor's question was for the guest to start telling the story Will was telling all over again. The tale began to layer and churn and fold in upon itself.

Now, Will was so high that we couldn't tell if he was repeating himself on purpose, or if he was just so stoned that he couldn't remember what he was going to say next. Dude was hysterical because he was so nonchalant about the whole damn thing, acting as if he didn't know why the whole group was laughing so hard we were pissing ourselves.

We were in fucking stitches.

At some point, someone asked, "What happened next, Will?"

He paused dramatically, as if trying to recall, and then started the bit with the news anchor all over again, as if this were the first damn time he was telling it. My sides ached, I was laughing so hard. At one point, I had to stumble away from the firelight to recollect myself for a second.

Will's cyclical story-telling was the highlight of that night, at least until Jack Scatterfield eclipsed it with his antics. His back to the fire, Jack began rummaging around trying to find something in the leaves at his feet. As his young hands sifted through the dry leaves, the puffy black back of the American Eagle coat turned toward the flames. Spontaneously, in a burst of light, flames leapt onto the black coat, eating up the thin synthetic material. Down feathers floated all around him.

"You're on fire dumbass!" Red yelled to Jack.

Jack flapped like a madman at first, unsure of what to do. In the partial darkness of the fire, he appeared to me a giant bird, rising from the flames, molting off small white feathers on the wind as the flames billowed.

Red grabbed Jack and threw him to the ground, rolling him until the flames extinguished. Jack rose up, onto his feet again, cursing and laughing and spitting feathers all at once.

Someone helped Jack shed what remained of the coat.

"You want it so much, you can have it!" Jack laughed, as he fed what remained to the hungry flames.

The fire roared up as it consumed the rest of its meal, sending more feathers floating, raining down like snow, in all directions. We all looked as if we had just wrestled down some giant white bird. In a way, we had. Jack had killed the American Eagle and emerged a phoenix.

From that night on, Jack was known as the Phoenix. He would rise from the ashes many more times in the years to come.

The most extreme example of the Phoenix's ability to evade the hands of Waverly happened a few years later, along a stretch of road I've already mentioned in the course of these episodes. Jack just finished assembling his newly modified chopper, and took her out for a spin. He wanted to open her up, see what she could do. The Phoenix rode south through the town of Groverton, stopping at the lights and keeping to the posted speed limit as he rode.

Once out of town, the Phoenix hit the throttle, really opening her up. He shot like a speeding bullet, south down the state highway. With no helmet, the wind whipped at his finger-length brown hair. He hunched lower over the controls, aerodynamically. Night wind whipped at his face. Adrenaline flowed.

Without warning, a nut shot off a bolt, and the forks fell away from the bike. As the forks failed, the bike miraculously launched the Phoenix into a cornfield, where he sustained some broken bones and a serious concussion, rather than being smeared in a mangled red mess across the road.

He was hospitalized for a few days, but walked away from a wreck that would have taken others down. That's what happens when you're a phoenix, and the wind knows your name.

the fountain of youth

We were on the cusp of the year 2000, and media hype began to swirl around fears of what the new millennium would bring. Anxieties ranged from computer glitches and Y2K to misread Christian and Mayan prophecies. Imagined chaos and worst-case scenarios poured down in the form of radio and television waves, washing the planet from satellites on high.

But I was 16, turning 17 within the week. I had the powdery evergreen slopes of Colorado to contend with, and reunited revels with Brett Damkott, a friend from years passed, stood in the foreground. Nervous anticipation flooded my veins when my parents hugged me and put me on a plane to the Rockies, my first solo flight and a remarkable amount of freedom for a kid of my age. My heightened senses took in every inch of the experience. I slid into a window-seat so that I might watch the country unroll like a scroll beneath my gaze. Strapped into the belly of this steel bird, I was off to see the world and get the hell out of Waverly. When the Rockies finally slid into view, my grey eyes lit as I took in the light and shadows that played upon the mountainous terrain below. Despite the unimaginative name, there was an inherent charm and magnetism in them.

Our plane coasted above the crests and, shortly afterward, down onto the tarmac. Our graceful descent from the sun-drenched Colorado sky elicited an altogether new "high" for me. Our bird landed smoothly across the paved land, as a steel swan unto her native haunts. My soul floated above, until the engines reversed, bringing my consciousness back down to the gritty earth. I took in the rolling hills as we taxied over to our gate.

Trevor and Sonia, Brett's parents, arrived to pick me up from Denver International Airport and we stopped to grab a burger at a restaurant near the Coors Brewery, which I could see towering in the distance, out the front picture window. Brett described how the brewery used mountain spring water to brew their famous beer. All this talk of beer made me thirsty.

Brett's dad bought me a Fat Tire ale and we grabbed a booth to catch up. I sipped at the frothy beverage reverently. Trevor, a six-foot balding dad with a perpetual glint in his eye started in on giving me shit:

"So mommy and daddy let you leave the nest? A big-boy trip. What's next?"

I just laughed and sipped my beer. I had no good comebacks. Trevor was like a second father to me.

Back in middle school, I spent almost every weekend at Brett's place, over in Huntertown, IN. We dove from the diving board on their back deck into the green waters of the pond behind their house, splashing and floating around in the summer sun.

I thought of their pet parakeet, who whistled the Andy Griffith theme song on repeat in the loft above their living room. I often thought to myself that someone should teach that bird another song. We were allowed to use Trevor and Sonia's hot tub when they were out for the night. I also had fond memories of Brett's crazy little sister chasing me around their yard with a kitchen knife, threatening to stab me if I didn't kiss her. One time Brett and I had found his dad's stash of playboys when we were snooping around looking for his mom's stash of weed.

It was no secret among our friend group that Sonia smoked. She was intense, the most high-powered mom I knew. Her hair was close-cropped and sexy, not the typical midwest mom hair. Pearls often adorned her neck. Her normal get-up was a business dress with a matching sport coat. At that point, she was one of the top saleswomen in the country for a haircare company, and was so good at selling the shit that she was always hosting parties and get-togethers at their place.

Other parents shied away from her in public for fear that she would hustle them into spending money they didn't want to spend. There was truly no shame in her game. I had incredible respect for that. She was always on some kind of health kick too, which prompted moans and groans from Brett and his siblings. Sonia was a heartfelt marijuana advocate. She would have been a hell of a black market saleswoman for that! Nowadays, she could push the stuff legally in Colorado and several other states. Indiana ended up being too conservative a place for the Damkott family, a larger-than-life, active family of free spirits, entrepreneurs, and big ideas.

After a hearty lunch at the burger joint, Trevor and Sonia left Brett and I to wander around the town of Golden. We caught up, filling each other's ears with all of the news. We hit a few shops, always coming back out to those sun-bathed sidewalks. We eventually ended up in a sports bar where a football game was being shown on the big screen. Brett wanted to watch. He was bigtime into sports, and was a natural-born athlete. I attempted sports for a few years, because if you were a kid in Indiana, that's what your parents thought you did. But ultimately, I couldn't give two shits about sports. I just didn't get all the hype about throwing a fucking ball around.

We realized when we sat down that it was St. Patrick's Day. The bartender informed us about the special on green beer. Even though it was just Coors Banquet Beer with green food coloring, we ordered a pitcher and continued to shoot the shit and watch the game. We both had fake IDs by that point. Brett had mailed mine over to me. I was Sean Ripley, from Buena Vista, CO. Brett was Conner Wilson, also of Buena Vista. The bartender eyed us suspiciously, but on seeing our IDs brought us the beer. I was wearing a Pink Floyd shirt with a huge psychedelic sun on the front. Brett was wearing a Nets jersey. As much as Brett dug sports, I dug music. A scruffy guy at the bar, probably in his early twenties, noticed my shirt and struck up a conversation with us.

"Nice shirt, bro! Love Floyd, man! I've never seen that one! Where'd you snag that?"

"Thanks brother! I ordered it from a Britrock t-shirt catalog! They have a much wider selection than any store I've ever seen."

We shot the shit with the guy for a while and he ordered us another pitcher of the St. Paddy's Day special.

A nice, heady buzz was underway. Colorado was treating me well...only a couple of hours and we had already partaken in two great establishments and killed two pitchers of emerald beer, brewed less than a mile down the road. I was digging Colorado. Coming from the bleak middle March weather of Waverly's cornfields, I felt like I was seeing the sun for the first time.

Later that day, and several days that followed, we hit the slopes of Breckenridge and a few other spots as well. I skied and snowboarded in those days, as did Brett. We had some great powder snow, and I don't remember much about the boarding, just that slicing through the powder was glorious. Even taking a spill on those slopes felt like falling into the hand of God. We got into this routine of boarding during the day, and partying during the evening, into the night. One night we stayed over at the house of a girl Brett knew, Jennifer. He was trying to hook up with her best friend, Maia. I ended up rolling around in a sleeping bag with Jennifer most of the night. I had caught a little cold, and had to keep wiping my snotty nose on an old t-shirt in the dark, for fear of snotting the hell out of her...but we made it work. Desperate times call for desperate measures…

The good times had to come to an end at some point, though, and we definitely ended them a bit prematurely, on one wild Golden night. Brett and I decided to go joy riding with one of his older friends, Kev, who drove a large blue and white Bronco - the boxy kind in which O.J. fled. Brett insisted that we hit one of the drive-through liquor spots, which we proceeded to do. No argument there. We each selected some spirit with which to start the night's frivolities. Brett was taking down straight Svedka. Crazy bastard. Somehow I ended up with a drink called Gold Schlagger, a harsh, cinnamon flavored beverage that had little gold flakes swirling throughout. We rode the hills of the Golden night, with gold flakes hoving in my belly and in my hand. Late 90's hip-hop music issued from Kev's stereo. The night began a gradual descent into fuzziness as the gold-flaked liquid went to work upon my awareness. Bass thumps to the vocal stylings of rapper DMX added a spice of adrenaline to the night. I schlagged that Gold Schlagger alright, and at some point snagged Brett's vodka, which I began to drink like water.

At some point, Kev dropped Brett and I off at an outdoor mall. For the rest of the story, I must defer to Brett's account, since I blacked out the minute I stood up to get out of Kev's Bronco. It was a cool night in the outdoor suburban plaza, near the majestic stucco storefronts. Clusters of young people congregated here and there across the parking lot and expansive sidewalks. The pillars of the place were uplit, and tropical plants spilled over the side of their concrete planters.

According to Brett, a significant swagger laid claim to my stick legs, and I could be heard uttering some of the most random and hysterical shit that he had ever heard me say. It's a damn shame the night took those words from me. I wish I was there to see it, hear it, and feel it, but alas I was somewhere else - God only knows where. My body was possessed by the alcohol, adrenaline, and the altitude.

We made our way through the yellow-striped lot, over to a group of Brett's friends and acquaintances. They were standing in a little cluster by an elaborate concrete fountain, which shot water tranquilly up into the night air, catching the water again in its underlit basin. Assorted silver and copper coins glittered up through the water, catching the light. The moon peeked out from behind the stores, watching over her children of the night.

The plan had been to meet up with Brett's friend group, and then stroll over to see a movie at the theatre down the way. That plan didn't pop off though. Something set me to singing and saying some poetic shit, and just acting a general fool. I was playing the role of Mercutio after the Capulet feast. Brett should have pulled me away saying,

"Peace! Man, thou speakest of nothing!"

But unfortunately, I was too far gone to be stopped. At one point, in the middle of my rambling nonsense, I had climbed atop a concrete ledge of the fountain, to address the good people around me. I lost my balance, falling head first into the fountain. Normally, a good splash of water in the face will bring someone back - sober them up a bit. This was not the case that night. Brett dragged my wet and wasted body out of that cold fountain water, while someone phoned for an ambulance. I was unresponsive. Soon enough the sirens snatched me up from the concrete and onto a stretcher.

I awoke the next morning to the beeping and whirring of monitors all around me. Trevor was there, waiting, as any good father would be. I knew that look of concern on his face, the scrunched brow, the beads of sweat along his balding head. He wasn't angry, just worried as hell. Here he was responsible for someone else's kid, and that fool had gotten drunk and almost drowned. The doctors and nurses had pumped my stomach while I had been in some odd state of temporary nonexistence. I rolled over, only to feel a sharp, stabbing pain in my right arm. There was a stint in my arm, giving me fluids, easing my teenage body back to the land of the living, not unlike Montag's faded wife.

A catheter had been inserted into the side of my penis, I soon found out. How can I begin to describe urination, post-catheter? Every time you go to urinate, the sodium in your urine hits that open puncture wound and you howl in excruciating pain. With each urination, comes a stabbing pain, like that of a jagged point...I coached deep breaths into my lungs for fear I might pass out and wrack my head upon the toilet bowl.

The Rockies impressed some limits upon me in those small hours, I nestled in a well-prepped hospital bed. The fountain of my youth had been found, and the pain was much indeed. Rather than grant me immortality, this fountain bore it away, granting me a keen awareness of just how mortal I was. As fate would have it, my time to be taken had not yet arrived. At the hands of first responders I was preserved.

It wasn't like me to get blackout drunk, but I guess the night got good to me and I had decided I could drink like Thor and the gods of old. And like the gods of old, I left a bit of my starry-eyed immortality there within the fountain. Most throw change into such fountains. I took change out.

Once I was able to pull myself together, by means of some toast and coffee and some Advil, Trevor, Sonia, Brett and I went out hiking in the Golden hills. My head still wasn't one hundred percent, but the fresh air was good for my spirits. No one need speak of the night before. They, perhaps, knew that lectures would be lost upon me. My issues hung in the air like a palpable presence - not so much an elephant in the room, but the thunderheads of an approaching storm. Clouds hung over the valley, creating shadows through which I must pass. When I returned home, I was grounded yet again. My parents set up a payment plan through which I could pay off my ambulance ride using the money I earned at the Grille.

white nonsense

I met Kaleb through the Scatterfields. Both his dad and the Scatterfields owned lake cottages up in southeast Michigan, so on our lakefront excursions I often ran into this cocky character. Up on that lake, we built fires which lasted for days, along a curving lakefront road. And somehow the alcohol always continued to flow. Granted, it was usually watery beer like Labats or Old Milwaukee, but it still amazed me nonetheless. When I first saw Kaleb, he rolled up in his dad's 1984 diesel Mercedes. He was smoking a Gold & Mild cigar and blasting Master P, a regional rap artist. Kaleb had that magnetic craziness characteristic of kids that don't want for anything.

At sixteen or seventeen, he was taking us out in his dad's speedboat, which he or Red Scatterfield drove. Kaleb and I became fast friends, so exciting and unpredictable did life become in his presence. I never met Kaleb' mom, but I do know that Kaleb had a close relationship with his dad, who ran a successful maintenance company in Mount Comfort.

Occasionally we water-skied or tubed, but usually we just wanted to take the girls out and fly across that sea of green glass. Sam and Jade were regulars in our entourage. Their light-hearted laughter kept our party vibes on the level. I began to date a girl named Kat, who regularly came up to the lake with her brother Karl. Kat and I would sneak off to swim under the willow trees along the lakeshore. The sensations of skin on skin, beneath the summer lakewater, away from watchful eyes, revved up our hormones and hungry hands.

Nick and his girl Hope often joined us for our evening swims. He and I had always been attracted to different types, but our young love lives often ran parallel. Where Hope was slim, pale, red-haired, and mild-mannered, Kat was voluptuous, tan, and high energy. Needless to say, Nick and I never had to worry about common love interests. While Kat and I's intense relationship didn't last too long, Nick and Hope went strong for years and years. Everyone assumed they'd get married once they'd escaped Waverly High, but things eventually fell apart. Kat and Kaleb would eventually have a few kids together and then split. I never could have foreseen that match back then.

The lakefront parties were mellow compared to the gatherings which graced the ranch. When the Scatterfield parents were out of town, showing horses, crowds filtered out onto the ranch. Cars lined the half-mile drive. Coolers the size of trash cans held beer and wine coolers. One never knew what they would get when thrusting their hand down into those ice-filled bins. I began to see Kaleb at those parties too.

He was neck deep in cocaine when I met him up at the lake, though I had no way of knowing this at the time. He and I began spending numerous mornings in his Ford Ranger, roving the countryside, smoking herb, dropping Lucy, or using dead presidents to vacuum up the occasional line before school. I have fond memories of riding high through the countryside on freshly-fallen snow, rapper Spice 1 on the stereo.

I recall senses at peak awareness, hillside homes, evergreens with snow upon the boughs, and Ja-Rule on the stereo. But, as interesting as the cocaine high was, I quickly determined it to be a bit too intense for me. I did not find it addictive whatsoever, but somewhat annoying, as it made my teeth clench and put me on edge. I was a fairly high-energy kid, and wanted mellowing, not amping up. Nevertheless, K kept the good vibes going.

Once, on Lucy, we saw flaming cars pass us on every side as we doubled over in laughter at the beautiful and chaotic cacophony of sights and sounds. Another time I remember waiting in the majestic stillness of a winter lot, smoking a small joint, as Kaleb ran in to "settle up" with his dealer, who had been hosting a shroom tea party. This, of course, made me picture Alice and the Mad Hatter, and the whole bunch.

His powder habit gradually escalated to a few hundred dollars a day, by the time he was a junior in high school. I soon realized this and, in a matter of months, watched him grow increasingly desperate for quick cash. His demeanor had grown more serious and pensive. He began to cook up his own crack, converting the powder and smoking the stuff. I joined him once or twice, but didn't take to it. He eventually got so desperate at one point that he walked miles literally in the snow to steal cash from his own cousin's house. Waverly was quick to fill his hungry need, as she nibbled away at his young frame. The dusty stuff blew in on all sides of him, forcing him into a corner.

But the real trouble started when the addict robbed a gas station where Jared's brother Zane worked - how much dumber can you be? Zane and Kaleb had been friends since eighth grade. Kaleb's dopey ass had marched into Lovington's Corner Store late in the evening, that dark blue Nike hoodie pulled up over his head. He wore a ski mask, and his grey Ford Ranger idled out back behind the building, thumping "Ambitionz as a Ridah" by TuPac.

Kaleb never had an actual gun - thank God - but his right hand, nestled inside the pouch of his hoodie formed the shape of a pistol. Zane laughed it off at first. Then, when Kaleb remained insistent, Zane grew serious and tried to reason with him.

"Give me the cash in the drawer!"

"Bro, are you serious?"

"Do I look like I'm joking, man? Hand over the fucking cash!"

"Alright, bro." Zane muttered, ejecting the cash drawer, flipping up the respective clips for each type of bill, and sliding them across the scuffed counter to Kaleb, who was growing increasingly agitated.

Kaleb was obviously too snowed out of his mind to listen to anything remotely resembling reason. With cash in hand, Kaleb hit the door running, peeling out of the tiny Lovington's parking lot, his grey Ranger heading northbound on the state highway nearby. As Zane watched the taillights of the Ranger fade down the street, he picked up the phone and punched at the worn numbers.

Waverly's finest rolled into the parking lot a few minutes later. The police station was only about a block north of Lovington's Corner Store, after all. One cop stood with hands on hips, asking questions, while the other took notes as Zane filled them in on the masked bandit of Waverly. If it wasn't so sad, the situation was actually quite comical. Zane knew everything about Kaleb - from his dad's address in Mount Comfort to his mom's place north of Waverly. Zane knew his regular haunts and, and probably even the location of the nose candy dealer. But Zane wasn't stupid. He gave the cops some basic info on Kaleb, including the address for his mom's place. Zane didn't let on that he knew Kaleb quite as well as he really did.

All of us were in the process of learning a valuable lesson: never trust an addict. When you speak to them, it is the addiction talking, not them. The real self is tied up somewhere deep down, buried under that snow drift. As predicted, Kaleb did eventually make his way back to his mom's house that night. When he did, Waverly P.D. was staked out and ready. They apprehended Kaleb without incident. They recovered a small amount of cash and about an "eight-ball" of substance.

Kaleb's dad hired some high-powered attorneys from Mount Comfort and, in exchange for a list of names (including mine), Kaleb got a slap on the wrist. I'm not sure what the actual charge ended up being, but it wasn't armed robbery…

Earlier in the evening, before Kaleb hit the gas station, he had tried to get me in on the action too, holding out two ski masks, and asking if I wanted to run a holdup with him. His eyes lit up like a little kid's on Christmas. I chuckled, and climbed into the passenger seat,

"That's a hard fuck no," I said, nonchalantly.

I told him that I didn't mind partaking in some petty crime, like breaking into a pop machine or something, but armed robbery was another level. Kaleb thought that was a great idea. Breaking into a pop machine was an easy score of a few hundred dollars. And who was really hurt by it? Pepsi? Coke? That was laughable.

We ended up hitting two pop machines in the parking lot at Waverly High. I stayed warm in the Ranger, acting as a look-out while Kaleb worked at the lonely machines with a crowbar. Between the two machines we got $300.

"You didn't even grab a drink?" I chuckled.

He threw the truck into gear and sped off. Once we turned onto the nearest country road, he tugged the ski mask off and tossed it into the small back seat. I counted the cash, but let Kaleb keep it. I had my job at the Pinehouse Grille and was making plenty for a high school kid in those days.

Kaleb dropped me back off at my place, and then headed on to rob Zane at Lovington's corner store. Out of all the gas stations in the area, why Lovington's? Maybe he forgot Zane worked there? Who knows how the mind of an addict works?

Betrayal is a fucking rude awakening, I was realizing as I sat beside my embarrassed parents in that county courtroom. Kaleb and I had been running together not all that long - maybe a year. Kaleb knew the words to every track by every '90s rapper, and as we listened to the songs, he would rap them out, altering the words to fit the passenger. I remember one specific day, rolling up to a stop sign by Shooster pallet company, Kaleb singing Pac out of his open tinted window, substituting my name into the song, personalizing on the fly and for the occasion: "Jay's got ki's comin' from overseas…"

Well, Kaleb closed that chapter decisively when I received the summons to appear in court. And in the courtroom on that slow, grey Indiana afternoon, Street Commando Kaleb became nothing more than Cokehead Kaleb to me - someone I might eventually find on the streets of Waverly or Mount Comfort, begging for cash. I ran my fingers through my wiry brown hair. I cursed myself for ever trusting an idiot like Kaleb. When he got picked up for robbing that gas station, his feet were put to the flames. He handed over a list of names to the police in exchange for a lesser sentence. He "rolled" on us - everyone around him.

When I went to court, my bluish-grey teenage eyes met the hazel eyes of a female judge who was finishing her lecture on the type of company I was keeping. Six months probation and 40 hours of community service. Damn. How fucking humiliating.

At the prompting of my mom, I completed a good deal of my community service at the local homeless shelter. Maybe she thought it would give me some perspective. Inside this beige stucco building, I witnessed Waverly's outcasts and addicts in full force for the first time. So this was where Waverly kept her untouchables, tucked safely out of the way, one block away from the police station. Though I considered myself a pretty non-judgemental kid, I had great difficulty looking the temporary residents of this establishment in the eye rather than staring at their torn and tattered clothing. Several of the residents eyed me curiously when I passed, this young kid in stonewashed jeans, concert t's, and dreads. I nodded to them in acknowledgment.

One Saturday morning, I shook hands with Joshua, the caretaker, who had rough hairy hands that betrayed many years of manual labor. Joshua thanked me for coming to help out. He asked me why I had community service.

"Got mixed up with a cokehead, who started robbing stores in the area. When he got arrested, he threw me under the bus."

Joshua nodded understandingly. "Well, there's a good chance that if your friend doesn't get his shit together, he'll end up here."

"Is there like a program for recovering addicts or something?"

"Yeah, we have a couple drug programs here, but they're underfunded and understaffed. And when the clean addict finishes a program, they go right back out to the same Waverly streets they came from."

"That's fucking depressing."

"Yeah, Jay...you said your name's Jay, right?"

I nodded.

"We're essentially a purgatory, Waverly's waiting room for the unfortunate, insane, and addicted. People are here for a hot meal and a roof over their head while they decide if life's still worth living."

"Surely there's more money somewhere for better programs."

"Oh, there's money, but Waverly has her priorities. We're pretty far down on the list. Close to the bottom of the list actually."

I contemplated this as Joshua walked me through a list of chores to tackle. Cleaning bathrooms, washing windows, mopping floors, tidying up the grounds. When he checked in on me at one point, I was wet-mopping one of the large hallways.

Raising his eyebrows he complimented my work, saying, "You can really handle a mop. You don't see too many kids with a good work ethic."

"Yeah, I'm kind of a perfectionist. I work down at the Pinehouse Grille, and put way more effort into that job than school. Just seems more practical. It's hard to focus on school when you don't really know where all of it is leading."

"That's understandable. Hey," Joshua said thoughtfully, rubbing his unshaven chin, "Would you like to help me out with a little construction project?"

"Yeah, that'd be cool. I did some construction work when we were having our house built. Anything that wasn't worth subbing out, and was pretty straightforward, my dad paid my friends and I to do."

"Alright. When you finished mopping, come see me in my office. Don't forget to put up those wet floor signs."

"Gotcha."

Joshua and I then ripped up, and replaced the carpet going from the downstairs landing to the upstairs, pulling the old worn, tattered carpet and padding up with pliers, rolling it, and tossing in a dumpster behind the building. We popped all the old staples up with flathead screwdrivers and hammers. Then we cleaned the subfloor, before cutting and laying the new padding and carpet in place. We stood back and admired our work.

At the end of the long day, Joshua shook my hand and signed my community service form, giving me credit for twenty hours even though I had worked only ten.

"Nice meeting you. Take care of yourself, Jay, and steer clear of the cokehead. Misery loves company."

I thanked him and then walked over to my mom's waiting car, thoughts swirling in my mind. Our pup, Terra, welcomed me, licking my face and settling at my side. We drove off to the comfort of our 6,000 square foot home in the evening light of Waverly.

everywhere a sign

Jared's hands gripped the molded indentations of the mustard yellow steering wheel as we rounded a curve at significant speed in the dusk. Tesla's song "Signs" blared through the cheap speakers of the Chevy Nova. I studied Jared's profile from the back seat, where I sat with Zane. Nick Scatterfield sat shotgun.

I thought about the time Jared had gotten stomped at Saddler's party. Jared had taken that in stride, completely unphased. He possessed some strange, deep-seated pride that a simple insult or ass-kicking couldn't touch. I had to respect that. I got to know Jared much better since we worked together at the Pinehouse Grille. With a calculated acceleration and a swift jerk of the steering wheel to the right, the sign came into view, then was mowed down, crunching beneath the car.

"The trick is to line up the sign with the hood ornament," Jared shouted loudly over Tesla's acoustic anthem. "You don't want to wrap that shit around your axle."

"Why are we doing this again?" I laughed, chuckling into my fist and passing a lit "pinner" joint to Nick up front.

"These signs are fucking up our city, Jay." Through thick glasses, Jared's gaze met mine in the rearview and he smirked.

Another calculated swerve and a metallic crunch. We bumped back onto the road. The song ended. Some lame song started playing. Jared reached down to change the tunes. I noticed the Nova was gradually crossing the center line. Another car came around the bend. Jared didn't seem to notice. He was still messing with the stereo.

"Bro!" I shouted. "Car!"

He swerved back into his lane, barely missing the other driver who was laying on the horn. I breathed a sigh of relief.

"Damn, bro. Let Nick handle the tunes. I'm not trying to kill anyone tonight."

Zane started laughing goofily and Jared smirked back at me.

"Chill, bro. I got it."

Another calculated swerve. Speed limit sign flapped down and crunched. This sign-smashing became a regular passtime for Jared, which he always continued for about a half hour, at intervals, until he got bored and wrapped it up for the night.

On other cool, clear nights, Waverly mixed for us a different cocktail of danger and delight. Adrenaline stood by, waiting for our embrace. We assembled in my parents' half-mile gravel drive and prepared to surf. In our brand of car-surfing, one didn't stand up vertically atop the car, as one would if they were on a board riding a wave.

We didn't have a death wish, just wanted a cheap thrill. The car surfer positioned themselves squarely on the roof of the car, as if he or she were paddling out to ride a wave. Both the driver and passenger side windows were rolled down. The car surfer stayed in this paddle-out position, gripping just inside of the roof of the car, curling their fingers into the car through the open windows. A level of added safety (if you can use that term for such an activity) was added by having the car surfer brace his or her feet securely against the frame of the back windshield. The number one rule for drivers during a car surfing episode was: NO SUDDEN STOPS. The car surfer would do a double-tap on the roof of the vehicle when ready to surf. The driver then shifted into gear and sped off into the night.

This ritual began with Kaleb, Jared and Zane, but continued with the extended crew. It was a tried-and-true adrenaline rush. We became seasoned surfers. The Scatterfields, the girls, and I perfected the activity, becoming more methodical in our calculations of wind, weather, and moonlight. Jared typically drove, so sensitive was he to the conditions of the road. We started putting more thought into the routes we chose for the endeavor, the best hours of evening.

Our rides could be seen careening through the northeast Indiana night, the tangled tresses of Hope or Jaquie or the others flying straight up into the night, as if being tugged by the gods. The heads of the riders would pop out of the vehicle occasionally, catching a kiss from the wind themselves, while observing the surfer. The moon often smiled down, lighting our way across the paved county roads of Waverly.

In those days, we rode many-colored cars through the night, as we were riding time into uncertain futures. We didn't know where we were headed, nonetheless, we rode the crest of each moment to its climax and trough. Negativity rarely showed up to rain on our insane parade. Car surfing continued for many years, with several iterations of participants. I have nothing but fond memories for the days of car surfing, feeling the cool wind tugging roughly at every follicle on my scalp, the night air pounding me in the face, the smell of the night in my nostrils, clothes, and lungs. Sometimes I imagined letting go, and being sucked up into the belly of the night. Of course, I wasn't dumb enough to try it or I wouldn't be sharing this with you right now. We were just Indiana teens drinking adrenaline and riding the wind through Waverly's night.

My alltime favorite memory of Jared grew out of a day not unlike all the other slow and predictable days at Waverly High. I had just gotten to my locker for the day. I was unpacking some books and stowing them on the top shelf of my painted red locker. I was bullshitting with Thompson, a girl a few lockers down. She and I had a regular banter we threw back and forth during the groggy morning influx of students.

"Jay, will you please cut those damn dreads? They're giving me anxiety. I keep thinking some bug is going to fly up out of there."

"Thompson, please wash off that clown mask. I'm not going to ask again. You're freaking me the fuck out."

It was amidst this back and forth that we gradually noticed raised voices and students accumulating down the hall. We broke off our banter and wove our way through the crowd. I saw the back of a white undershirt and long brown hair with close-cropped sides. Craig - a recent transfer from Mount Comfort. He was confronting Zane near his locker. Accusations flew back and forth.

"Zane, you say'in I slept with Heather? I wouldn't go near that slut!"

"That's not what she says, Craig. I get my info from the source."

"Fuck your source."

"Sounds like you did, Craig."

Then fists were flying. They were bouncing off lockers, from one side of the hallway to the other. Chanting bystanders grew lounder, feeding off the adrenaline of the moment. Fights weren't that common at Waverly High. At first, there was no clear winner, but Craig managed to land a few shots squarely on Zane's jaw. Teachers migrated toward the mayhem. I moved in to restrain Craig. I went in under the right arm and across the neck, pulling him back. He started throwing elbows, trying to toss me off. I pulled him off Zane, whose lip and eyebrow were cut and bleeding significantly.

"Chill bro, I cautioned. You're good. You made you're point."

"You'll regret this," Zane swore, wiping his face.

Craig pulled forward, and then began to settle as I relaxed my grip. Mr. Soddermeyer helped Zane up from the floor. Gordo waddled into the crowd, dispersing them by the sheer fact that only so much physicality could occupy a certain space at a given time. Students migrated away, back to the regular routine. Soddermeyer nodded a thanks to me for helping to shut things down.

Red had found his way over to me and asked me for a rundown. I gave him the play-by-play. He nodded as I fed him the events.

"You know we have to tell Jared," he sighed.

"I know bro. I'm dreading the fallout."

"Better sooner rather than later," Red warned.

The tardy bell rang. We marched through the halls toward Jared's first period class. We asked to speak with Jared for a minute. The teacher allowed it. We explained the situation and watched as Jared started to fume. If there was ever "a bull in a china shop," here he was.

"Where is he?" Jared demanded.

"Main office," said Red.

Jared walked off with a purposeful gait, toward the office at the other end of the hallway. He was wearing blue jeans as well as an untucked navy and tan flannel shirt. He rolled up his sleeves as he got closer. He pushed his glasses up on the ridge of his nose. Shit was going down. I had to half run, half jog to keep up.

He threw open the plexiglass door before Craig could get his bearings, pulled his out of a chair and started slamming fist into face. The shocked secretaries were fluttering around the room like fairies calling on the gods of force. Jared knocked Craig over a half-wall, and then went around and picked him up to reignite the fight. Craig managed to get a few undercuts in, which only infuriated Jared even more. They were knocking papers off counters and bumping into machines.

Red and I watched with delight. In came principals from every side. We rushed into the vortex of flailing bodies and arms. Red and I tugged at shirts and pulled at limbs, making a show to break up the feud. We got in a few guts shots on Craig for good measure too. Gordo came flying in from one of the halls leading into the main office, only to bounce off the scuffle and land on a potted plant, crushing it entirely.

Finally, finally, the blows settled down. We backed away from the fray. Red and I received pats on the back and were sent back to class. But at least we knew that Craig had been handed his ass.

the igloo and the elephant choker

Some days just assemble themselves around us. The construction of the infamous Scatterfield Igloo was just such an event.

Each of us gradually greeted the morning at the Scatterfield pad. The Phoenix walked shirtless and sleepy-eyed across the hallway to take a leak. I had awoken early, as I often did, and was talking to Kathy at the kitchen table, over coffee. Benderbeast was at work by then, helping the robots at Glower Automotive to churn out those tires.

It snowed in the night, and Ben had plowed the driveway before he left. As we gradually assembled in the kitchen, the Scatterfields and I sat looking at a snow-covered landscape, unsure of how to make the most of the day.

I don't remember if it was Red or Nick that suggested an igloo. One of them had spotted the giant mound of snow near the trident arms of the drive. I think it was Red.

"I know what we're going to do today." He said, a gleam in his eyes, his fiery hair messier than normal.

I turned in his direction, raising my eyebrows.

"We're going to build a fucking igloo."

I laughed and rubbed my eyes. Kathy sipped on her coffee and stared at her excitable son, waiting for what would come next.

"Not out of ice blocks. Out of compressed snow."

Nick wandered over to the glass storm door, which looked out through the open garage. He pointed to the eight foot snow mound next to the drive.

"We get out the Bobcat. We add a little snow here, a little snow there, and then we pack it down real well from the top. Then we can carve out the inside."

Laughter assaulted me. "Let's do it," I smirked.

After suiting up, we began the endeavor. Red added some snow to the sides and packed down the pile with the bucket of the Bobcat, a small multi-purpose piece of equipment they used to plow the drive and move weighty items around the ranch. We selected a side of the pile for the opening. We took turns, chopping away with shovels, filling up five-gallon bucket after five-gallon bucket with snow. We were miners, mining our way to an experience. I wonder what Kathy was thinking as we chopped away at the mound of snow. I guess as long as we were on the property, her mind was at ease.

The whole process took a couple hours, with about four of us working in shifts. After we had completed the steps Red had laid out, a makeshift igloo sat before us. Red and Nick snagged a piece of wood from the shed and fashioned a sliding door, which could be raised or lowered.

We stood back and took in our masterpiece. We felt a bit of the pride that the great ice sculptors must feel. We had stolen a home from the wastelands of Canada, and plopped it down in the Indiana morning snow.

"Call the girls?" Red asked.

"Call the girls. Nick confirmed."

Hope, Jaqueline, and Kat showed up shortly after we called. The max capacity of our igloo was about six people at a time. The inside was a large, somewhat cramped, icy oval. It sat four comfortably, but it was dark. We brought in some flashlights and lanterns. The experience was somewhat primal, like that of being in a cave. Jaqueline was losing her shit over the igloo.

"I can't believe we're in a fucking igloo...in the middle of Indiana. You guys, we're about to smoke in - an - igloo!"

She was cracking me up. We broke out a bag of leafy green buds. Whenever one of us was well-stocked, we all were well-stocked.

"Bring in the Elephant Choker?" asked the Phoenix, ducking his head into the structure.

Nick affirmed the suggestion using his signature thumb and pinky hand gesture. Jack soon retrieved the Elephant Choker from its case inside. The Elephant Choker was invented by Nick Scatterfield. It was a greyish-green gas mask, which had been modified. Where the air-intake normally was, a foot-long transparent forest-green cylinder extended. A small steel bowl, about an inch in diameter was mounted atop the cylinder, to be packed with Waverly's finest greens. The far end of the cylinder was wide open, allowing the toker to cover it with one hand until the chamber filled with smoke. Once the chamber was filled, the hand on the end could be removed, releasing all the accumulated smoke up into the lungs.

In this way, minimal oxygen was inhaled, and maximal THC fumes. The "Choker" part of its name came from this effect on the wearer. Even one round with the Elephant Choker would set seasoned smokers, choking and coughing hysterically. This "choking" effect, mixed with the lack of oxygen, set the stage for an intense and dramatic high.

Our igloo only added to the effect of the Elephant Choker. Here we were in an ice-age sweat lodge, breathing nothing but first and second-hand aromas of the herb smoke. I think our longest round lasted only about 20 minutes. At that point, we crawled from the igloo's mouth, as if she had just birthed our stoned asses into the mid-morning snow. The last one out still wore the Elephant Choker, and stood coughing bravely in the morning sun.

Smoke still issued forth from the mouth of the icy structure, billowing into the future.

sean ripley and the white hen

As you've heard, I was able to acquire a "fake ID" from Brett Damkott by way of Colorado. I turned the plastic card over and over in my palm, eyeing my photo with the false name. I peered at the Colorado seal, which was etched lightly into the background. On the seal was a crossed hammer and pick-ax, and above that a mountain range - the Rockies.

Ultimately, we were all mining life for something in those rocky days. I was mining down through the absurdity, trying to reach those pearls of wisdom. Little did I know how much time I would later spend in those Rockies, further up the range at a military school in Montana. The all-seeing eye looked out from its triangle at the top of the seal, sunrays emanating in all directions. This unnerving eye seemed to gaze out into my future. There was a bundle of birch sticks, tied up with a battle ax. I would need this battle ax in years to come, to chop through uncharted territory. With the birch twigs I could start a fire to warm my soul in the cold days of hell to come, or build a hideout in the hills. On a banner below the images of the seal were the words *nil sine numine* - nothing without providence.

This id was of regular use to myself, and my crew. A good luck charm. Several days a week, I made lunchtime liquor runs, up to Waverly's small liquor store - The Party Store. On my first visit, the clerk, Roy, eyed me with suspicion, glanced back at my ID and shrugged. I shot the shit with him, asking him for bar and restaurant recommendations in the area. I explained that I would be in the area for about the next year or so with FiberOne, a company out of Colorado laying fiberoptic cable. I borrowed this scenario from the Scatterfield Boys, who actually did lay fiberoptic cable in the summer and on weekends. I think the store clerk was just happy to have the conversation or the business.

I became a regular there, grabbing my signature "Beam and Coke," then running down my list to grab other items for those in my crew. I put hundreds of dollars through that liquor store in those days. My price was cheap. I only asked that kids buy me a drink of my choice when I went to grab their order. In this way, I drank for free throughout much of high school. I was a regular, and once a regular, always a regular in a small town. I popped in around the noon hour every other day or so to,

"Hey Sean, what's good?"

Kids could regularly be seen tipsy in the halls of Waverly High. All this fun lasted for but a season, until that unfortunate day when the Great White Hen swallowed Sean Ripley whole.

It happened in that windiest of windy cities, Chicago, where I was on a weekend trip with my parents, who had allowed me to bring one friend. Nicky Scatterfield was along for the ride.

We toured the John Hancock and visited the Museum of Science and Industry. My parents decided to go out and explore near our downtown hotel. This left Nick and I to hatch new schemes in the big city.

"What should we get into while the parental units are out and about?" Nick asked, brushing his blonde hair out of his eyes.

"I saw a sports bar downstairs yesterday afternoon," I said. "Let's start there."

We had a few beers and watched a little of the Cubs game. We paid, and made our way out of the bar. On our way to the front lobby of the hotel, we took a wrong turn and ended up in a corner store called the White Hen Pantry. Browsing its contents, we found rows of refrigerated bottles along the back wall.

"Let's grab some Bacardi Limón and mix ourselves some drinks." Nick suggested.

I contemplated the suggestion for a second. "We got time?" I asked.

"Sure," Nick said.

"Okay," I agreed. "Let's do it."

We walked around, nonchalantly, as if making tough decisions. I settled on some cheese, crackers, and a bottle of Bacardi Limón. We carried our contents up to the checkout counter, where a friendly Arabic man began to ring up our contents. He paused abruptly and asked for my ID. Dumbly, I removed the card from its sheath in my wallet and handed it to him.

Normally, I would have just flipped my wallet open, and showed the ID through the clear photo slot in my wallet. Why I removed it that day, I'll never know. He glanced at the date on it, and was about to hand it back, when something seemed to catch his attention. He looked closer, raising it near his face. He picked up the phone and began to dial.

"Is there a problem?" I asked.

"Do you have any other IDs?" He inquired, his friendly smile now a stony frown.

"That's my driver's license," I replied. "It's my only ID."

He finished dialing. "Yes. I got a fake ID over at the White Hen on Cicero."

Nick and I bolted for the door to the street. The store clerk slammed down the phone and attempted to come around the counter after us, to no avail. The guy was boxed in by his own orange rectangular counter. He fumbled with the latch toward the back of the counter. We burst out of the White Hen, like two insects that had scampered free of its beak. Out of the corner of my eye, as I burst onto the Chicago sidewalk, I noticed fake IDs plastered to the front window. *What an idiot I was! Had we only entered from the street!*

We sprinted left, down the crowded sidewalk. A few doors down, we swung into an sleek charcoal colored office building, and ran right into the mouth of a waiting elevator. I had seen *The Fugitive.* I knew what to do. I punched the number thirteen. The doors closed swiftly, moving us upward smoothly and efficiently, in the direction of the thirteenth floor. The elevator smelled of freshly waxed tile and stainless steel polish. The doors opened to a slate-tiled hall with artificial potted plants. A man and a woman in business attire passed us in the hall, not seeming to notice us. We were beyond the bounds of their business banter. We walked briskly down to a glass door, which opened onto a rooftop patio. We walked over to the edge and looked down.

A CPD squad car sat in front of the White Hen. We ducked our heads back, away from view. We plopped down into some patio furniture which dotted the rooftop patio. My eyes met Nick's blue eyes, as if to say, *That was a little too close for comfort.*

Once we recovered our cool, we talked for about 30 - 40 minutes while we waited for the smoke to clear. When the time came, we traveled back down to the ground floor, back out into the sidewalk crowds, in the opposite direction of the White Hen. We walked around the block and entered our hotel from the grand front entrance. When we stepped back into our hotel room, Nick and I exchanged knowing looks. We had had our fill of adventure for the time being. Us small-town kids were not ready for the unforgiving world of the big city. We had a moment of silence for Sean Ripley, who was now in the belly of the Great White Hen. Luckily, the hands of providence had delivered us back to safety.

the drunken armada

Young hands drug aluminum and red fiberglass canoe bows across the pebbled shore of the Mongo River. The sun kept pace in its steady ascent beyond the trees, glittering down magically through the leaves. Our fleet began to assemble. Canoes sat perched on the banks, ready for launch. Coolers were stocked with groceries and libations. Skin glistened in the morning sun, as hands squirted sunscreen into palms and lathered up the backs of friends. Some girls stood bare-breasted, nipples perked up in the morning breeze, while others opted for the stylish support of colorful bikini tops. Admiral Sparks handed me his Newcastle bottle, which I held as he tied a red bandana across his brow. A smaller version of myself stood reflected in the lenses of his aviator glasses - a small dreaded figure with shades. Sparks stood upright, bandana in place. He looked like a pale Hendrix.

Nick tossed me a banana, which I promptly peeled and began to eat. He and I shed our shirts and drug our canoe down into formation. Nick pulled out a joint, lit it, and passed it to me. I took a drag, held in the smoke, and passed it on, to another outstretched hand. Red Scatterfield stood in his canoe, ready to shove off. He put his sandaled foot up on the prow, threw his fist up in the air, and shouted, "Viva la Mongo!" He was a hippie George Washington, his fiery hair in the mid-morning sun, his freckled face leading the forge. In the back of Red's canoe sat a stoic-faced Jared, a Honey Brown beer in hand and paddle at the ready.

One by one, canoes shoved off, grating against the pea gravel of the riverbank. Noses turned downstream. Nick sat at the head of my canoe, blonde hair glistening in the sun, and I at the stern. I watched his paddle dip into the water expertly. I balanced out his pulls with my own, on the opposite side of the canoe, and we shot forward, into the translucent green waters of the Mongo. We paused, letting ourselves coast, as I produced a fifth of bourbon whiskey. I took a guzzle and passed it off to Nick's outstretched hand. He passed me the joint, which had somehow made it back to our canoe. Skunky aromas hovered in the air above the river, held in by the trees which crouched protectively on either bank.

As my paddle again dipped softly into the stream, I wondered how our Native American counterparts must have looked on a similar day several hundred years back. Wooden canoes, most likely...and flowing raven hair. I watched as small water striders scampered across the surface tension of the water, away from the drunken revelry, heading for calmer waters. There was a commotion up ahead. As Nick and I drew closer, we saw that a canoe had flipped. Jared and Red splashed in the water, light-heartedly accusing each other for tipping the boat. Jared's thick glasses had been lost in the scuffle and they were waiting for the waters to clear so that Red could extract them from the Mongo. Another member of our crew waded into the middle of the clearing, cursing upon discovering that his pack of cigarettes was drenched. I chuckled to myself. Nick and I maneuvered around them and continued downstream.

A canoe of girls pulled up alongside us. We clinked bottles and shouted "cheers" to the morning sky. They produced a cantaloupe, along with a few watermelons. Knives were produced. We carved up the melons, passing slices around. Cantaloupe and watermelon juice ran down our chins as we sank our teeth into the slices of overripe fruit. We threw the rinds out into the bushes on either bank.

Sparks and his shipmate cruised up to our cluster.

"You're really nursing that whiskey today Chapparal," he prodded.

I accepted his challenge, holding the bottle up to the sky, inspecting what was left. About half a bottle. I tipped the bottle to my lips, tilted it back, and guzzled for a couple minutes as a grinning Sparks watched. Others chatted obliviously. When I had sucked the rest of the golden brown liquid down, I screwed the top back on and threw the empty bottle near his canoe, splashing him.

"Nurse that shit!" I responded.

He just smirked, grabbed the bottle from the water, and threw it on the floor of his canoe.

"Crazy bastard," he laughed.

Some canoe-hopping occurred. Coupling up transpired between various members of our entourage as our initial sobriety was washed away down the Mongo. A few canoes shot temporarily up small tributary creeks, far enough for a little privacy. Occasionally, a giggle or cry of pleasure wafted out from the trees. Those still on the main river rose up whoops of cheer in response, as the armada sailed on downstream.

At one point, something below the surface of the water caught my attention, possibly a fish or a unique rock, glinting in the sun. I leaned closer to inspect it through the water's rippling surface. Cries of laughter erupted as my body tumbled overboard into the Mongo. My head popped back up to the surface, a look of shock and surprise on my face. I flung my sopping brown dreads back out of my eyes.

"Going for a swim with old Jimmy Beam?" Red shot down at me.

"That was the slowest fall I've ever seen!" Nick chuckled, offering me a hand, and pulling me back aboard.

The jokes continued to flow as we paddled on. The newly drenched skin and wet trunks refreshed me as we continued on into the afternoon sun. I was now one with Mother Mongo.

Further downriver, canoes were beached. Members of the armada leapt from a small rock outcropping, into a deeper section of the stream. Jared had stripped down to nothing, and flung himself out into the morning air, his incredibly white ass practically blinding onlookers when it caught the sun. He appeared light as a bird, until gravity brought him crashing into the cool stream. Others joined in. They swam cleanly over to the side, like sleek and strange amphibious creatures. Others jumped, partially clothed into the flowing waters. Shorts, bathing suits, or underwear clinging to their bodies, supporting and concealing as they splashed into the emerald waters. The colorful pieces of cloth accented slim and chubby frames. The stretched fabric contrasted with pale and bronze skin as forms swam over to the bank, and climbed on up for another leap. Some jumped fully clothed into the lazy river, who quickly made it known that she preferred not the awkward sopping cloth, which impeded strokes and made short swims unnecessarily difficult.

Once we'd had our fill of leaps and lunges, we again set our course downstream. We revived the smoke, and bottles once again appeared. We alternated periods of intense paddling with periods of no strokes, or lazy strokes. Sometimes we rushed like arrows across the water, while at others, we crept silently and stealthily along, sneaking up on the afternoon like water moccasins.

During one stretch where we were coasting for a bit, Nick and I started waxing philosophical. So engrossed in debate were we, that we didn't see the fallen tree that lay across the river when we rounded a curve. The spent maple stretched from riverbank to riverbank, straddling the entire river. There was a crater where its roots had been yanked up from the earth. About three feet of clearance lay between the water and its horizontal trunk.

As it sped into view, I opened my mouth to say something. The canoe slid beneath the trunk, Nick's head struck the tree. His clothes-lined form spilled overboard. I reacted as quickly as possible, laying back against the canoe and holding my breath. The rough trunk grated up my chest, and across the side of my face, as I slid beneath it. My sunglasses crunched, and dropped into the water below.

Nick and I emerged scraped up, bruised, and cursing. Luckily, we were numbed up pretty good by that point in our journey, and were able to laugh about it within a few minutes. Red and Jared paddled up.

"You boys hittin' the trees again?"

"Clever, sir. Very clever."

I had some gnarly scabs from the bottomside of that tree, but walked away with my ego intact. It wasn't the first time, and wouldn't be the last time Mother Mongo would knock me upside the head.

The rest of that year's run was smooth sailing. The Mongo River flows out into an open lake. We paddled across, portaged around a small dam, and then base camp came into view.

After that inaugural run, the Drunken Armada became a yearly tradition, lasting for a good fifteen years after that. The group quickly ballooned. New names and faces appeared each year, alongside veteran members of the crew, but still Mongo flowed.

around the bend

I've heard some say the number of the beast is 666. Well, that wasn't the number of our beast. She was known by the number of those she consumed, a number which only went in one direction - up.

She was a hungry snaking right arm of Waverly stretched out across the countryside, miles west of town. And like a sleepy charcoal snake, she could go weeks or months between feedings. This strange reptilian road rose and fell, rose and fell, swerved abruptly to the left, swerved abruptly to the right, and continued on up through the cornfields and creeks towards my parents' estate back among the fields. The road claimed many lives by rising up unexpectedly, tossing vehicles into the mulberry trees which grew by her roadside. The first incident I recall was when she munched hungrily at Red Scatterfield's blue monster truck.

Nick, Red, and I stood staring at the crumpled cab of the Chevy monster truck, glass shards embedded in our dripping and bloody hands. Nick had a sizable gash along his left temple. The truck lay upside down in the middle of a right angle curve. The cab was crunched down pretty badly, but the hood and rear end still looked otherwise pristine, like a calm and sparkling blue pond in the Indiana afternoon.

Red had insisted I take a turn driving the monster. Nick had taken a turn on a long flat stretch, and Red wanted to give me a chance as well. I at first protested - I did not yet have my license. But with some prodding from Red, I soon relented.

This elbow of the county road was a paved right angle turn, coming from the east and curving to the south, a sharp, banked section of road. A gravel road branched off to the west. Tall pasture grass bordered the road on all sides. Assorted gravel lay scattered across the intersecting curve - a recipe for just such a disaster. When I hit the curve, the tires couldn't gain traction. They spun and screeched, spun and slid, until the truck seemed to launch itself up and away from the road. Time slowed down.

Being inexperienced, I panicked, stomping on the gas and brake simultaneously. I heard the slow grating sound of folding, crunching steel. I found myself hanging upside down, behind the steering wheel. Red was riding shotgun. He also hung in the air like a disappointed tourist on a bad rollercoaster ride. His red hair hung down from his suspended, freckled face. Nick was in the back seat, wearing no belt. He had been tossed around like a rag doll from side to side. Blood streamed from a cut above his blonde left eyebrow.

The engine was still running as we hung suspended by the safety belts. Red reached over and calmly turned off the ignition. The windshield had shattered, spraying glass in all directions with a pop, but most of it had settled below us on the inner ceiling of the truck. The only option was to gingerly press our hands up into the shards of glass, unbuckle our safety belts, and tumble out. I got out of there like a bat out of hell. I had seen too many action films and was afraid the damn thing was going to explode.

Red had spun out on the same curve earlier that morning, landing the truck in the ditch. I wasn't as lucky or experienced as Red. As the three of us stood there, roughed up by the reality of it all, I just kept apologizing like an idiot. I offered to pay him back for the truck if he gave me a little time to save up the cash. I told him I understood if he never wanted to chill again. I apologized over and over and over again. All the shit I was saying just rolled off his shoulder. I wonder what was going on in his head.

"It's just a fucking truck," he said turning from the wreckage and making eye contact with me and throwing a bloody hand over my shoulder.

We all burst out laughing. I knew he was making light of it for my sake, but he also had enough chill to let shit like that roll off.

We then turned and walked south, toward my parents' long gravel driveway, which was about a hundred yards off. My parents were still at the church's fall festival, so we let ourselves into the house and cleaned up a bit. We washed our hands and picked out the tiny pieces of glass. It turned out none of our hands were cut as badly as they looked. So much blood from such small wounds…

Waverly's finest showed up and filed a report. Red said he was driving. (I didn't have my license yet.) The police were understanding. They said we weren't the first to wreck on that curve. We probably wouldn't be the last.

Eventually, I helped Red, Nick, and others rebuild that truck. We've remained friends throughout all these years. We've had many other good times in that blue monster, but we learned to take the turns a bit slower. What a chill guy!

"It's just a fucking truck."

In preparation for publication, I was discussing my account of this event with Red Scatterfield. He shared something which shed new light on this event. He informed me that Benderbeast had purchased the truck from a fellow factory worker. The guy had torqued up the truck for intense off-road excursions. He had made several performance modifications that resulted in the blue monster being incredibly powerful. When this guy found out that Ben's boys would be driving it, he recommended that Ben tune down the engine of the blue monster, removing most of the aftermarket modifications, so that the boys didn't kill themselves if they ever took it out to "really see what she could do." Benderbeast took this guy up on this recommendation, remodifying the truck so that it had a reduced amount of power available to the user.

I sat back and reflected on this new information Red was sharing with me. The ripple effect of this random guy's decision to be vocal to Ben gradually washed over me. Had he not said something to Benderbeast, maybe we'd all be dead. Or even worse, maybe we wouldn't be dead, but paralyzed or in a vegetative state. Maybe I'd have to live with the thought that my reckless actions had killed a friend. I shivered at these thoughts. The guy could have just taken the money for the truck and called it a day, but he didn't. He did more when he could have easily done less...Why? This random guy showed a remarkable amount of foresight and empathy by caring enough to say something to Benderbeast. The fact that Ben took the time to listen to this random guy is significant as well. As I write this in the year 2020, I do find that hindsight is 20/20. The pieces begin to fit.

Waverly's favorite meal was painted steel and fiberglass. A close second though, were young and unsuspecting adolescent frames.

Another acquaintance, Chis, had barely escaped Waverly's bowels. Along one of her s-curves, she had risen up, flipping Chris's Red Thunderbird end over end over end. The vehicle came to rest upside down in a creekbed, leaving him dazed, water washing through the windows of the broken car. Her creek babbled carelessly through the dead Thunderbird and Chris' busted dreams. His thick hands unbuckled and tugged himself free of the wreckage just before she swallowed the car whole. He stood there along the creekside, watching bug-eyed, mouth agape, as she consumed his polished pride.

For a time, Waverly amused herself by throwing birds into the path of Sam's approaching car. This period didn't last long, but was one of the oddest things we saw from her. Waverly hurled large birds - chickens, pheasants, and wild turkeys - up into Sam's path. One day it would be a wild turkey, the next a murder of crows. The dents began to accumulate on the hood and bumper of Sam's new ride. Feathers lodged themselves stubbornly in her grille. During this period, we dubbed Sam "the birdslayer" because she consistently mowed down everything Waverly threw at her.

The heat and crickets droned on in the fields. Sam and I bounced along in a tan Lincoln Towncar, driven by a chubby kid named Johnny. We had just scored a couple ounces and he was giving us a lift back to my place. We didn't know

Johnny all that well, but he was one of many occasional herb suppliers. Sam and I floated along in the back seat, her long straight hair whipping me in the face.

The Dead's Terrapin Station echoed through the towncar speakers. We let ourselves be lulled into a false sense of security by the hum in the summer air. We had sparked several bowls by that point, and were still savoring our highs. But Waverly was growing hungry, seeking satiety, and she began to squirm. We headed down what we thought to be a tame stretch of the road, a gentle rise and fall. We bumped smoothly along the tar path, which glinted in the sun.

Without warning, she threw us up, over a rise. A tractor crawling down the road a hundred yards ahead. The driver - a ten year old kid in overalls - craned his neck back. Johnny, in a split-second assessment of the situation, thought the tractor driver was pulling off to the right to let us pass. While the tractor driver was swerving out to the right, it was in order to make a wide left turn.

The inertia of Johnny's speeding towncar left him no reaction time. The green tractor lurched right into our path. The smooth hood of the tan towncar folded up between the thick dark wheels of the tractor. The shocked face of its kid driver stared down through the windshield of the towncar which had plowed into his ride.

Sam and I reached impulsively for the long chrome doorhandles, the only thing between us and the open air. Our young hands tugged and stepped out onto the tar-coated road. Wildly, Johnny's hand fumbled around under his seat.

"You guys get the hell out of here," he said, shoving a bong, a gun and other paraphernalia into Sam's mirrored hemp shoulder bag. My mind started racing.

He knew there'd be cops, and likely a search of the car. Sam and I exchanged frantic glances and started to walk northward toward my parents' house. The depth of our ignorance about Johnny's past quickly rushed in on us. The weight of the fallout from our missteps began to creep into consciousness. Why the fuck did he feel that a firearm was necessary? We were in no concrete jungle. What kind of people were we running with?

For a time we jogged, feeling the uneven spine of the county road under our feet. We headed up a rise, and then down the other side, curved left and then right. I threw the glass bong off into the trees, and heard it crash as it met the bark shell of a hawthorne. I checked to make sure the safety was switched on, and tucked the gun under my shirt, and into my belt.

We turned up a gravel drive that belonged to a kid from school named Adam. We knocked on a door. A woman's face appeared at the door.

"Could we, by any chance, get a ride to my house?" I asked. "It's just north of here, about a mile. Our friend has been in a wreck down the road and is waiting with the car. We don't want our parents to worry."

"Is your friend okay?" Adam's mom asked, concern apparent in her voice.

"He's upset about his car," we told her, "but other than that, he's fine. He's waiting for the police to come."

"Adam, honey, watch your sister. I'm going to give these kids a ride back home." she instructed, grabbing her purse and keys from the laminated countertop.

"Thanks so much, ma'am. You're a lifesaver." we heard ourselves saying.

By then Waverly had surely consumed what was left of Johnny's towncar. We made small talk as the mother's car turned back onto the blacktop, and headed north toward safety, away from the wreckage. Sam was chatting it up with the sweet woman, as I was distracted by the deathstick that was lodged near my belt. My mind raced with scenarios, prepared for contingencies. Sweat formed on the young hair at the back of my neck. We should lay low for today, and ditch the weapon tomorrow, I finally decided.

We pulled up to the tan brick facade of the Chaparral residence. My parents were out. We thanked our good Samaritan, who then pulled away down the dusty drive, and turned south. I ran in to hide the small ebony handgun. I had no idea the make and model of the thing, just sensed it was toxic to the touch. Sam phoned her parents and told them what she could. I handled the pistol as if it were poison, as if its sheer deadly potential could melt off my hands. I stowed it away inside a cinder block basement wall.

A sheriff's cruiser eventually pulled into the turn-around in front of my parents' house. A heavyset uniformed officer in a tight-fitting tan shirt stepped out and adjusted his hat, leaving the cruiser idling. He strolled easily up to our door, pushing the doorbell with his calloused finger.

I made eye contact with Sam, waited a minute, took two deep breaths, and flung open the large door. Sam stepped up by my side.

"Hello officer," we greeted. "What can we do for you?"

"Hi there," he started, smiling a patronizing smile. "Were the two of you just in an accident down the road?" He inquired.

We confirmed that we were. He looked over us and then chewed on his lip.

"Are you aware that leaving the scene of an accident is a crime?"

I exchanged glances with Sam. She brushed her hair behind her ear.

"No sir," she cooed. "We just wanted to get home so our parents knew we were safe."

His eyes studied us again. "Say, aren't you Steve's daughter?" recognition spreading across his face.

"I am," Sam laughed, modestly.

"Why didn't you say so?" the sheriff chuckled, rhetorically. "I thought I saw the resemblance. No cuts or scratches?" he asked with concern.

"No sir," I said. Sam shook her head, innocently.

"Alright then," he said. "In the future, if there's an accident, be sure to remain on the scene." We both nodded, promising that we would.

"Hopefully, there won't be any future accidents," I said.

The officer smiled, and then turned to leave.

"Thanks for checking on us," Sam offered.

"Just doing my job," the sheriff countered, over his shoulder.

In this way, we avoided death on Waverly's roads yet again. Her hunger was temporarily satiated, and our skins were temporarily safe. I was starting to think that a false sense of security was the only sense of security there was…

The next day we drove by Johnny's dilapidated house in downtown Waverly and threw his piece into a large burning bush out front. I phoned to let him know it was there, then deleted his number from my phone. Neither Sam, nor I ever spoke to Johnny again. I wanted no part in messing with someone who ran around packing.

Smoking and being a general shithead was one thing, but running around strapped was another. We were trying to catch a buzz, not a bullet. We weren't down with that. We swore Waverly would never catch us off-guard again. We approached her with intense caution from then on.

a raincheck

I had about fifteen steaks sizzling on the open grill at Pinehouse when Jared's giddy face popped around the corner. I had just added more Hickory chunks to the smoker trays and was tidying up my grill area.

"Hey, what's up bro? I didn't think you were on the schedule for today?" I prompted, rotating a steak to create the Pinehouse Grille's signature crosshatch searmarks.

"I'm not, Jay. Just wanted to see if you or Moreno wanted to go for a little joy ride. Just got that engine rebuilt and I was going to take her out on the backroads to see what she can do!"

A little black box on the counter spit out another ticket: 6 oz. sirloin. I flung open the narrow stainless steel fridge door, sliced open a six-pack of sirloins, and tossed another on the grill with the aluminum tongs.

"I'd love to, man, but I'm closing tonight. I'm sure Rob would probably let me off early, but I'd really like to keep those nice fatty checks coming."

Jared frowned, and then lit up again when he caught sight of Moreno's stocky frame headed towards him, with some spent dishes from the buffet.

"Come show me the way to the next hippie bar…" Moreno intoned, placing his bearlike palm on Jared's shoulder.

"What about you, Moreno? Want to go riding?"

Moreno smirked, tossing the empty stainless steel buffet dishes into the dishwasher's area. His long black hair was pulled back out of his eyes. He wore a hair net.

"Nah, Jared, man. I'm closing tonight with Jay."

Jared looked like someone stole his puppy.

"You guys are going to make me go riding a-lone?"

I laughed at his persistence.

"Sorry bro. We'll have to pull a raincheck on this one."

Jared smirked.

"Alright. You're loss!"

Jared made his way to the back door of the restaurant, next to the giant janitorial sink which Rob had once used to spray his drunken ass. Jared exchanged remarks with a few other friends who were on shift that night. I heard his rebuilt gold Chevy Nova peel out into the July night, and he was gone.

I had finished that grill shift uneventfully. My parents picked me up. I showered, and fell into a deep, restful sleep.

I awoke to my mom, holding the phone in one hand, shaking my arm with the other.

"Call for you," she said. "It's Kat. Sounds urgent."

As I have mentioned, I was dating Kat at that time, a very chill girl who hung out with our whole entourage. She was as much a friend as a girlfriend. It wasn't like her to get worked up about things. I reached out my sleepy hand for the phone, yawning.

"Hey Kat, what's up?" I said sleepily.

"Are you sitting down?" I sat up, tossing my legs over the side of the bed.

"Yeah," I managed, groggily.

"Jared's dead," she said, pausing for the news to sink in.

I rubbed my sleepy eyes, my mind attempting to process.

"What?" I said, the news not computing.

"Jared's gone. He was thrown out of his Nova last night when it wrecked. He was headed south on a county road and I guess he lost control when he came up over one of those hills... I guess he was going pretty fast. They think he was going about 90. No seat belt."

I was silent for a long minute. I could hear Kat breathing on the other end of the line.

"Holy fuck." was all I could manage.

"I don't know what to say," Kat whispered, breaking the silence.

I could tell she had been crying.

"He stopped by Pinehouse last night. To see if Moreno and I wanted to go out for a spin. We both had to close, so we didn't go. Holy shit..."

"I'll see you soon, Jay." Kat whispered, hanging up.

I sat petrified in that single bed. Gone? What did that even mean? How does someone just up and disappear from your life? Erased from existence...

Who would tell the Scatterfield boys? I wondered. They were in France for the summer. I rang up Benderbeast.

"Hell-o" came Ben's voice on the other end of the line.

"Hey Ben, this is Jay. Did you guys get the news about Jared?"

"Yeah, Jay.... We can't believe he's gone. So tragic... I feel so bad for Zane."

"You going to let Red and Nick know what happened?"

There was a pause.

"Kathy and I think it would be better to wait until they get back in the states to break the news...We don't want to ruin their trip, and there's nothing they can do about it."

The funeral was a few days later. Everyone who could come was there. The majority of the Pinehouse Grille staff was there, including our manager Rob. I think half the town of Waverly was there, the parking lot of the Seller & Park Funeral home was bursting at the seams. Cars were parked in the grass since the lot was full. A bunch of our crew rode together. I saw Moreno and Crystal, whose eyes were tear-stained, failing at their attempt to appear stoic.

On my way up the front walk, I spotted Jared's little brother, Zane, looking off at the rolling clouds in the distance. It was like he was searching for Jared up over the horizon, but he wasn't finding shit. I went over to him. We wore black suits. We never wore fucking suits. Suits weren't our thing. He eyed me, angry tears welling up in his young eyes.

"Hey Jay," he said, his voice cracking.

My voice caught in my throat. I couldn't think of one fucking thing to say as I stared into those sad puppy dog eyes. What do you say to someone who has just lost their older brother - the person they looked up to most in their life?

"Hey bud," I whispered, reaching out to give him a hug.

He lost it then, starting to shake and cry on my shoulder. I stood there with him for a while, somewhat awkwardly absorbing Zane's tears.

At some point we made our way inside. I rejoined the group, and sat down in the rows of identical padded chairs. How many rituals of death had taken place in these cheap seats, I wondered.

Jared's casket was laid out up front, flowers and wreaths surrounding it. Jared's mom stood nearby, looking lost in that nice dress she had never worn, somehow preparing to put her first-born son in the ground. The closed casket said all there was to say, I thought. Jared was gone. Case closed. No redemption, no reprieve...Snatched up and smashed on Waverly's backroads...

I don't remember what anyone said during the service, some standard salve to ease the pain of loss and fear of the unknown. At one point, they put on a playlist of Jared's favorite songs. We all lost it. I was sitting next to Kat and Sam. We all started blubbering like idiots, tears and snot running down our faces. We flooded that funeral home with our tears. Through the rain of tears a familiar song: "Kryptonite," by a band called Three Doors Down.

When the song cut through the speakers, I felt Jared speaking to us from the other side. He was leaving his body lying somewhere in the sands of Waverly. She would consume him. He looked on, unable to change his fate…

Waverly's nails wrenched the emotion from our guts. She had swallowed our brother whole…this kid who was the closest thing to Superman his family knew...

I felt a part of my innocence slipping away as Jared lay all packaged up that day. Up until that point, I think we all felt a bit invincible. We stared at the reality before us.

What kryptonite did Waverly clutch? What allowed her to eat up that positively quirky, hard working, and loyal kid from us?

Ambition? Curiosity? Innocence? No one knew. Silence was the only answer we got. But his death did, in fact, put many of us back on solid ground.

There were no more illusions about our mortality. This fragility of existence met us head-on. What force had saved us from the same fate?

On that last ride, Jared soared through the windshield of that gold 1969 Chevy Nova, breaking his neck instantly when his body landed in the empty cornfield, Waverly's threshing floor. Years later, I found out what "nova" means in Spanish: "It doesn't go." Damn, I thought. Ain't that the fucking truth... everywhere a sign...fucking up our city.

Years later, Zane started a band which he called Icarus Falls, in memory of Jared. I went out to see them perform a few times. Zane was the drummer, and they were actually a pretty decent indie rock outfit. They held it together for a few years, even recording an E.P. Unfortunately, over time, Waverly doused the band in alcohol and arguments, setting it ablaze. She's one cruel bitch, eating men like air... I had to get the fuck out of there. When Waverly gets to snipping threads, she really cuts it up.

Last I heard, Zane was hard at work with his uncle's septic service, sucking up shit for a living.

lucy for days

Lucy came to me through Lucas Habergast, a lanky waiter at the Pinehouse Grille. Luke's royal blue Pinehouse polo clung loosely to his frame as he took orders and ran plates to booths. Unbeknownst to all but a few, Luke had access to large quantities of Lucy, which his brother concocted in their unfinished basement. Luke had been tasked with discovering new outlets for this black market med.

Small towns always harbor a handful of street chemists, and Waverly was no different. Of course, some are con artists, the equivalent of snake-oil salesmen, but others possess a genuine skill in this unlawful science. Luke's brother fell into the latter category. Sorting out which is which can sometimes be a difficult task, especially given the lack of regulation. Suffice it to say that like most small businesses, the clients of the street chemist rely on word-of-mouth referrals and testimonials from friends.

At that point, I had tried Lucy once or twice with Nick, and had enjoyed the "trip" or 8-hour long flow of hallucinogenic visions. When I told Luke I was intrigued by the prospect of becoming a distributor, he began to patiently and expertly field my questions. On our ten-minute "smoke" breaks from our Pinehouse Grille posts, Lucas and I began to iron out details. He offered to sell vials of 100 doses to me for $100 a pop. I could then turn around and sell individual doses for $5 each, making a $400 profit on each vial of the potion.

In the cafeteria of Waverly High, I assembled a "meeting of the minds" to lay out a potential Lucy pyramid scheme, and discuss how such an operation might play out. Around those laminated cafeteria tables, amidst the cacophony of adolescent voices, we hashed out a carteleque scheme among the major distributors in the school. The major distributors would get bulk discounts from myself and a few others who were working directly with Lucas. We would only sell to these lower-level distributors, and to our close inner circles of friends. $5 would be the going rate per dose. If anyone was not satisfied with their experience, they would get their money back, no questions asked, with the caveat that they would never be able to purchase again. We wanted to run a clean business, with no bad blood, no unnecessary hostility. We were not unlike the perfectly legal pyramid schemes of our day. Not unlike Mary Kay or the Catholic Church, we peddled illusions.

We thought the setup was air-tight, promisingly under-the-radar. Lucas was a fit tennis player from a neighboring high school, entirely above suspicion. Neither he nor his brother were directly distributing to the public. They were the creators, we the wholesalers, and the lower distributors functioned as retail.

As Lucy began to flow through the veins of Waverly, things got weird. When I strolled around the halls, it was not uncommon to see wide-eyed kids petting the carpeted walls, running hands over the grouted tile, laughing hysterically at a mirage, or staring out at specters in space, contemplating other realities.

Operations ramped up quickly. The first week, we went through one vial: 100 doses. By the third week, we were running through several vials a day. Lucy is unique among substances, controlled or uncontrolled. While some similarities do exist, its shape-shifting properties set it apart. Since the product came to us as a liquid, it could be placed on virtually anything. The most popular form it took during our operations was as PEZ candies. At one point, it became commonplace to see kids with PEZ dispensers on every corner of every hallway. For $10, or two doses, students could purchase that round-trip ticket on the Lucy train. She took other forms as well...paper, sugar cubes, gel caps - you name it.

I later learned that PEZ candies were first marketed in 1920s Austria as a mint-candy alternative to cigarettes. Nowhere did these little candies live up to their purpose more than on the countless tongues of us Waverly youth...talk about a super-charged alternative to cigarettes...ho-lee shit….holyshit.

And the shit was holy, if approached with respect and reverence, but for most it was just another form of entertainment. I experienced both ends of that spectrum: the Doors of Perception and the Doors of Deception. The trip is easier to travel when you know which door you are walking through.

To me, the Lucy craze was a giant social and psychological experiment. Only time would tell how Waverly would respond.

a question of balance

Once a month, during the Lucy days, I would nestle into my walk-out basement room and test a vial myself. How else to proceed with quality control? Surely, I shouldn't be selling a product I wasn't willing to ingest myself.

Under the influence of Lucy, I rarely ventured out in public. Like an R & D department, I found that controlled environments were best for this sort of trial. Most of these monthly trips, I let the music be my guide. Every song, every album was a budding world, waiting to bloom. Ritually, I began every trip with Justin Hayward's poem on the track "Nights in White Satin."

Upon liftoff, in the purple hues and blacklight of my first solo trip, I soared right into the lines of reality. I had taken two doses, and sat sipping a tall glass of orange juice in my grey wicker chair. As my mind began to downshift, to hum and reel, a fluorescent violet, gridlike web rose up before my eyes. My corneas encased two ocular suns, rising up, bending new light on the first morning in a new land. My pupils continued to expand and adjust as this new dimension unfolded. Third eye began to open, casting off its sleepy encasement.

Time began to shift and slow, as my mind settled into that crossroads where light and sound intersect. My pupils began to eclipse their respective irises. The present moment was thrown open, beneath a microscopic lens. Once this new plateau was dialed in, equilibrium reached, the fluorescent violet lines of light slowly solidified the more I focused on them. In time, I would perceive this grid to be the web on which the world is hung, the multi-dimensional sketch pad on which realities are written. These are Lucy's diamonds, which she has spilled upon the sky.

The seeds had been eaten, attention and intention set, and the fruit was sure to grow. The lines of reality remain obscured unless we are in relative darkness (and I was at this point). These lines are also virtually impossible to see for the untrained eye, unless one focuses their attention on the darkness itself, looking into the heart of the darkness. Perception, I found, is conditioned. The substance was merely an aid in shifting my perception, for the first time in my young life at that point. Lucy was fracturing my perceptual patterns, ripping through the schematic blanket of prepackaged thoughts. Forgetting my learned tendency to only focus on the well-lit areas expanded my knowledge of the metaphysical fabric of the world. Through intense focus, I can now revisit the lines of this web whenever I wish.

In my monthly experiments, I would learn to recategorize Lucy-induced phenomena into either hallucinations or illuminations. Perceiving the lines of reality fell into this second category. I did not learn that what I saw were the lines of reality until much much later, after reading a significant amount of native American testimony and talking to a few others who had seen what they described as a net that held everything in its place. Carlos Castenada, for one, describes the experience very vividly in his book Journey to Ixtlan. It is a common experience for seekers to see these lines in a native American ceremony, such as the vision quest, whether with the aid of hallucinogens or fasting. Once again I must note that these lines are seen most easily in the shadows, in the places our minds and eyes don't normally care to inspect…

But I digress... I threw myself on my bed watching the notes and lyrics of my music blossom into scenes, my eyes losing focus, and then refocusing, an ebb and flow of my mind which followed the suggestions of the music.

Giant worker bees covered my walls, their golden, fuzz-laden bodies climbing over each other. I saw that I was seated in a hive of activity. Each bee went about it's work with diligence and attention to detail. I saw that maintaining the hive is an intricate task, much like building a shared reality. I tip-toed over and inspected them closely, in all their colorful detail: shades of yellow and black, clear rigid wings, large eyes calculating and measuring. I grew bold and reached out to touch a soft, carpeted backside. They paid no notice to my shadowy presence, but continued on with their busy work. How much are we like bees? All our feverish work to build and maintain our imagined communities…

Black widow spiders inched across my bare chest as I lie among my tangled sheets. First one arachnid, then another materialized from the painted walls. Soon they flowed out, coming in swarms, scampering in droves. I sensed they were my fears manifested.

Their tiny eyes searched and measured the silence, while I steadied my reeling mind, tottering on the edge of paranoia. With deep inhalations, my self-talk became comforting, reassuring, and calm. My nerves began to right themselves, allowing me to slice through irrational fears. *What look to be spiders, are a trick of your mind, brought to you by potions, chemical manipulations of thought.* Such words were repeated as mantras, until they seeped in. Storms were calmed, the sloshing waters subsided.

How susceptible the mind is to suggestion and manipulation! Peace was made with the skeletons in my closet, and in the murky waters of the unconscious.

Doorways shifted and sometimes disappeared. Strange spiraling portals arose, to worlds not yet seen. Shadows shifted across my window shade, manifesting fears of being chased, found out, or followed. SWAT teams repelled from choppers out in the dark, shifting shadows. Default fight or flight responses were disabled via logic. A calm inner voice carried me through until dawn: *Let's be reasonable here, Jay. No one cares about you or what you ingest. The U.S. Drug Enforcement Administration has much larger fish to fry than your little Lucy experiments*

Sometimes lush lusty gardens conquered my young soul, trips to tropics and their sun-bleached sand. Warm breezes, bare skin, and tropical flowers enchanted my mind. Hand in hand with a goddess, I walked down these new paths of pleasure.

Waves of sound washed me into these strange, alternative dimensions. Under the sway of two doses, the mind visually projects what it hears. So sensitive are the senses, shifted and rearranged at various angles and weights. A river of prismatic, auditory magic rippled through my soul. Holographic universes sprung from the seeds buried in the sound. The spells of word and sentence spun new poetic worlds... Old spells broken, new spells engaged...controlling what is perceived, and what is ignored - where our attention comes to rest…

As the Moody Blues sang, angelic figures draped in white cloth marched out of the darkness. Letters floating away like leaves on the wind, vanishing through the walls of my room. It was as if the vocalist narrated my internal monologue, externally... A well-dressed couple walking a city sidewalk, oblivious to my gaze. Yes, exactly. Amen. I couldn't have said it better myself. Yes, yes. Most of the people I know...faces flashing in and out of focus... The Moody Blues taught me poetry and perspective, much deeper, and subtler than I got at Waverly High.

They took me atop skyscrapers to witness taxi-colored beetles scurry across downtown streets. They took me on plane rides into the star-studded skies...up across swirling galaxies…

Under the sway of the Brazilian band Sepultura, I saw a spinning holographic Earth growing, rotting, dripping away and being reborn. Temporal cycles played out before my gaze.

Marilyn Manson, that sadistic prophet of the 1990s, performed holographic shows, suspended in the mid-air of my room. Long, straight, jet black hair framed his pale face and translucent chest. I met his piercing gaze, inspecting his mismatched contacts. In his left eye, only the pupil was visible, a dot of black against a pale, bloodshot sclera. The iris of his right eye glowed with a blinding violet light around its dark pupil. I sensed this pair of eyes was designed to unnerve - to trigger fear. Some say eyes are the windows of the soul. Well, these eyes were purposeful mirrors which conjured up long dormant childhood fears of monsters under beds and tucked in closets. Manson was all the murder and lust of America rolled into a character, and here he was. Shimmering halos of light encircled his face as he sang his song "Long Hard Road Out of Hell." I listened intently, attempting to empathize, but falling short. Such were some of the pain-laden thoughts which washed over me on those days and endless nights. I learned to hear, without judgement, and to contemplate what I'd heard.

Judgement is often second nature to us. Such judgement was absent from me on these flights of imagination. I felt the strings and sinew of my awareness stretch. I saw friends living fast, some dying young. Suicide was never an option on the table for us - myself or my group of friends. Thankfully, our times in hell were that of a shallower sort.

To be in hell is to know the dark truths of this world, and while heavy at times, this knowledge makes an even greater degree of joy possible. One can't possibly ascend to heaven unless they have dined with the dead, walked the halls of hell. The things we associate with the concept of hell are what make living and loving (things Manson said he wanted) possible. We should be, if not grateful for the gift of pain, at least aware of the dynamic, because it makes true joy possible.

Some songs, over which I tripped, spoke no truth, made no value judgements, but I experienced them nonetheless for what they were - unique and beautiful moments. Time reversed, folded and unfolded. Moments were compressed, expanded, then compressed once again. Shadows became any number of sights, one shifting into the next.

On one trip, a short stocky hombre, with a thick moustache, stumbled out from a desert, asking me questions in Spanish. I wasn't sure how to respond. I must have stared at him, turning my head, uncomprehendingly, like a confused pup. My Spanish wasn't too great in those days. He kept saying something about intelligence: "Tu no es inteligente?" He repeated over and over, in different tones, raising one eyebrow and wiping the sweat from his forehead with a folded red handkerchief.

On another trip, I rode the roller coaster waves of sound and light that issued from our furnace all night long. This was one of the most bizarre experiences of my life. What a swirling, shifting, colorful, lengthy ride on waves of mechanical sound. Like a mechanical lung, it pumped warm air throughout the body of the house, which could be heard to sigh and relax as oxygen flowed out to the extremities.

Amidst the black light, and darkness of night, all manner of sights unraveled before my mind's eye. Self-control and mastery over self were essential as I walked through these open doors, and down the halls of perception. All senses were in full swing at these times and I truly lived inside each moment. I unpacked these moments, living out the relative nature of time. I came to each trip with the intent to expand my knowledge of reality, to contemplate, to dig deeper. I was curious, and high school classes weren't cutting it. I was thirsty for experiential knowledge, not second or third, or fourth-hand information. It was with this childlike curiosity that I explored reality as seen through the colorful, kaleidoscopic lens of Lucy.

I think there is an important distinction to be made here. Had I come to each trip with the intent to escape reality, I may have walked away with entirely different results. Perhaps this is due to the fact that I was raised in a middle-class home and had a very stable home life...I'm not sure. I must also note the importance of personality differences in approaching anything.

a license to chill

Soon enough, it seemed that at least a handful of students from every group, every clique, were experimenting with the stuff. Of course, all this nonsense didn't fly under the radar of the administration for long. We were immediately alerted when questions started to be asked. Every seller had a plan on how to "lose" the stuff in his or her possession at a moment's notice. Some planned to consume it, flush it, crush it, etc. Strange tales began to crop up. We heard tell of a kid, a lower-level distributor, who, when pursued by Waverly's finest, had consumed all 50 doses he had on his person and then fled into a nearby cornfield. Supposedly, when he was found lying on his back among the rows, his mind was a blank slate. He had no idea who he was or where he had come from. Imagine that...a factory reset at age 15...hard drive wiped clean. You think you just dropped out of the sky into the middle of a cornfield...talk about a trip.

Eventually, my name did come up, either randomly or through some subtle snitchery. Admin questioned me for a few minutes:

"Jay, your name has come up as being one of the dealers behind this LSD epidemic. You don't seem like the type to use the stuff, but they say most dealers don't actually use their products...So we wanted to speak with you to see if that might be the case with you?"

"What's LSD?" I asked, scrunching up my brow quizzically.

The administrators exchanged glances.

"Maybe if you describe the stuff to me, I can be on the lookout for it, and let you know if I spot anyone using or selling it."

"Don't worry about it Jay. Thank you for your time."

I walked out of the office, ready to close down the entire operation at a moment's notice.

Later the same day, I had another close call. I had just settled into my basement room for the afternoon when my mom surprised me, telling me to grab my coat and get in the car.

"We're going to get your driver's license, Jay. I know how much you've been looking forward to it!"

I started to panic.

"Uhh...can we go another day?" I asked, knowing I had a short window before the stuff kicked in.

"What's wrong? I know how hard you've been working to scrimp and save for a car. You might as well start driving as soon as you can."

"Uhh...I just haven't been feeling great today."

"Oh Jay, I know you're nervous about driving, but you'll have to get over it."

"How about we get the license today, but I wait to start driving until I feel a little better?"

"If that's what you want, honey. I just thought you'd be more excited."

"Oh, I am excited. My stomach has just been weird today. I'd rather be on top of my game when I start driving."

"Okay Jay. I'll go grab the keys. Get your shoes on."

I was panicking, picturing a scenario similar to one my uncle had described from his hippie days...when he and his compatriots had all decided to do some chocolate mescaline, leave the commune, and go for a drive.

A few miles down the road, it simply vanished, leaving only beautiful green sod for miles in every direction. He had to stop driving, open the car door, and reach down to touch the pavement - to check back in with reality. Once he did so, he knew they were, in actuality, on the road, though to his mind it still appeared to be a luscious emerald lawn in all directions.

They executed a careful U-turn and proceeded back to the commune to ride out the rest of the trip in peace there. I wanted no such thing occurring to me now or ever, but especially not with my mom along for the ride.

I climbed into her maroon passenger van, and we had a silent ride into town, other than the James Taylor issuing from the van's speakers.

I managed to pass the paper test without issue. I had been studying for weeks. It came time for the bureau to collect my basic information, check my eyes, and take a picture. My mom still sat in the waiting area, reading a magazine.

"Height?" the lady behind the counter prompted.

"Five foot eight." I whispered.

"Eye color?" she asked, looking over the spectacles perched on her nose.

"Grey," I spat nervously.

"Grey?" she asked, confused. "They look black to me."

I could feel my pulse quickening. Black? Shit.

"I am fighting a little cold today. Sometimes when I take cold medicine, my pupils tend to dilate. My normal eye color is grey," I said decisively.

She bought it. Thank God.

"Now we need to check your vision," she cooed, motioning me over to a small screen. "Just put your forehead up against this pad and call out the letters as you see them come up."

I stepped up and bent over to look at the screen, pressing my forehead against the pad. Translucent birds flew every which way across the screen. Fireflies glinted here and there. Prismatic colors ricocheted from side to side.

Oh shit, I thought... Just focus on the letters, Jay. Ignore everything else, I coached myself internally. I read out the letters as I saw them. I kept reading.

"Well done," she piped, in a chipper tone. "You have great eyesight. 20/20."

"Thanks so much," I replied, somewhat bashfully.

I just wanted to get the hell out of there.

"Now if you'll just step over in front of this backdrop, we'll get your photo taken."

I obeyed, the flash sending sparks showering in every direction. I stared, wide-eyed and dumbfounded at the sparks falling all around me like golden snow. She eyed me warily, then printed out my license and handed it over the counter.

"Congratulations! You're now officially an Indiana driver!"

"Thanks again," I said, waving and trying to ignore some of the tracers and peripheral hallucinations I was starting to see. Golden glitter still seemed to rain all around, piling on the heads of other folks in the waiting room.

I flashed the license to my mom. She got up, smiled, and hugged me.

"I'm so proud of you, Jay! I knew you'd get it."

We walked back out across the parking lot to the car, me feeling like a shitty human being.

wake the dead

Our parade of insanity was, on occasion, graced by a kid known as the Hick from the Sticks. Whenever the Hick ventured out, events spiraled accordingly. The hedonic wheel of fortune smiled upon us. The Hick inhabited a bare-bones two-story cottage on the outskirts Waverly. Who were the Hick's parents? Some said they were doing time with the county. Others speculated that he had broken them up and driven them off with his unpredictable antics. He sported a close-cropped head of curly brown hair, a pale face pock-marked by pimples, and owned a wardrobe of Slipknot t-shirts, advertising a band who appeared to worship the noose. A perfect band for a man going nowhere...

One sunlit afternoon found me dropping Lucy with the Hick. I don't recall the circumstances that brought me to his humble abode, but there I was... He and I sat on rude wooden rocking chairs in his living room, which contained no other furniture. Light streamed in through the dusty horizontal blind slats, onto the scuffed hardwood floor. The room appeared to change and shift in the filtered sunlight. A single silver clock hung on the wall, above a fireplace teeming with spent black coals and ash.

The Hick and I watched as the seconds began to drip down from the clock, spilling onto the oak floorboards. This spilling-of-the-seconds awakened the floorboards, who, curling and straining themselves up from their respective nails, gazed sleepily around the cottage, taking in the strange upright creatures who inspected them. I froze in my rocking chair. Perhaps they wouldn't notice me. Uninvited fear filtered into my thoughts. Would they think I had cut them up and nailed them there? I watched the light ripple through their newly-animated woodgrain.

I had the impression of intrusion...that I was seeing something which was not for my eyes to see...something esoteric, forbidden. Time, dripping onto, or away from, the short-sighted, thoughtless works of man.

"Who has nailed you here?!" I cried, straining forward in my rocker.

Within the wood swirled mysterious patterns, not unlike those on my fingertips and hands.

"Fingerprints of God?! Have we sliced apart her hands?!"

I stood, hands nestled in my strawlike hair. I looked over at the Hick, locking eyes. A stupid smile appeared across his face, which, for some reason, angered me. He began to rock faster and laugh, hysterically, first softly, and then gradually louder. Finally, I could no longer endure the drip, drip, drip of the clock, or the piercing knotted eyes of those curious boards, or the Hick's insane laughter. Without a word, I ran over to the storm door, feeling the boards shift uncomfortably beneath my feet.

The fresh air at once began to calm my frantic mind. Once outside, I headed north, crossed the state highway, and walked slowly home through the newly harvested fields.

Such an experience is like a dose of heaven, and a dose of hell, neatly packaged. These are not places one goes, but psychological experiences or alternate dimensions of this current world. Take the melting time, and the frightful floorboards, for example... Briefly, I had sliced through time to something deeper - a small spoonful of the mystery and insight, the language of God - had been stamped upon my consciousness.

I had no conversations with snakes, but I did consume the fruit of the Tree of Knowledge. Though fearful, I gained insight into a deeper side of this garden we know as our shared reality. The dose of hell comes into the picture with the mental weight of these new insights. God is at home in wisdom, mystery, and insight, but I only had a small dose of that knowledge, and it was almost too much to bear. Sipping even a little of that knowledge psychologically isolates you from others in the garden of your shared reality. Surely this is a bit of what the prophets felt.

As native Americans have noted since they first encountered Europeans, our Ego is the most ravenous appendage. Greed is the water in which it swims. Ego is the engine which drives our economy and culture. With time measurement, we milk this garden, squeeze the most from every second. We harvest its forests, the sticky blood of its trees on the steel teeth of our machines. We separate and isolate ourselves from the reality of these acts. We wear colorful blinders. We mortgage our futures, and those of our children. And what do we gain? Thus it was revealed to me that God might live beyond the garden walls, metaphorically speaking. The fruit is the ticket out.

Spirits were on the move, adrenaline running high. The halfmoon of summer was hanging in the silhouetted trees. A crew of us piled into the crushed velvet seats of the Hick's plum-colored Buick, headed down the gravel road and out of town.

With windows low, the summer night wind rushed through the car. She ran her fingers wildly through our hair. Grey dust rose behind us as we careened through the blackness, a choking dust which settled on tallgrass ditches, and cornfields, and sleepy houses out of sight. One could not predict what the Hick might do, which is why most of us were along for the ride.

The Hick put the pedal to the floor, and then abruptly slowed, sped up again, then coasted. He repeated this frenetic acceleration and deceleration one final time as we approached a dimly lit sign on our right: Christian Union Cemetery it read. Nervous laughter issued from the girls, and whoops from the guys. The Hick cruised up into the first gravel drive, killing the headlamps. He hung out the window, manning the wheel with a clenched white fist in the darkness.

"Wake the Dead!" He shouted, abruptly, at the top of his lungs.

"Wake up! Wake the Dead! …Wake up!" he chanted.

"Wake the Dead! Come out! Come out!"

The halfmoon rose higher, straining herself to see this plum-colored boat of kids bobbing in the sea of the dead. At a fork in the road, between two large oaks, the Hick threw the car into park. He threw open the door and scrambled up one of the oaks, swinging from branch to branch, until he was about halfway up the tree in the darkness. The Hick hung away from the tree like a fucking newage tarzan, and began to howl. He howled up at the winking orb, attempting to coax her down out of the heavens.

I pushed the driver's seatback forward, which caused the seat to slide away on its track. I stepped out the driver's side door, which stood wide open in the moonlight. The others remained seated in the car, but readjusted themselves now that I was out. I produced a small, pinlike joint from my inner jacket pocket and sparked it with my blue bic lighter. I inhaled deeply, and exhaled, a couple short coughs issuing from my constricting lungs. Before offering the herb to those in the vehicle, I held it up in the moonlight, watching the small rope of smoke stretch itself up into the heavens. I pictured the Hick launching himself from the tree, catching hold of the smoke rope, and beginning to climb toward the wispy clouds. I passed the ganja off to an outstretched hand and walked off among the lichen-crusted stones...

Those days we worshipped adrenaline, especially when she flung us up against the sleepy walls of Waverly. When I look back, I'm amazed I survived half these endeavors which could have easily ended the flowering of a fragile life.

Perhaps the shape-shifting halfmoon put in a good word on our part, jesting with God. We were fruit not yet ripe, future wine for generations to drink.

"Who wants sour grapes? Give them time. Give them time," she may have urged.

For whatever reason, we were salvaged. She was not yet ready to press us for drink. We were too entertaining, is what I like to think. A hick, a writer, and company riding through the night...

the holy ghost

Nick Scatterfield called one afternoon, wigging out on Lucy. I guess he figured I could be his tripsitter, talk some sense into him. It wasn't the first time I'd talked someone down from a bad trip. Red had dropped him off at the public library while he ran some errands in town. As you'll recall, Nick was a colossal book fiend…

"Jay, Jesus is at the public library."

"Hahaha...what?" I laughed. This was going to be rich.

"So I'm at the library. I dropped two, man. Washed 'em down with Mountain Dew. I started wandering around, leafing through books. I came across a book of optical illusions. I plopped down into one of those big oak chairs with the high armrests and thick cushions near the back - you know the ones - and I leafed through the illusions, feeling the body buzz kick in."

"U-huh," I confirmed, pacing across the tan carpet of my room as I spoke.

"Well, I came to this page. All it had was a few oddly positioned black splotches on it. The instructions told me to stare at the collection of splotches for as long as I could without blinking."

"Right."

"Well, I did that and now the ghost of white Jesus is everywhere I look."

"White Jesus?" I asked, confused.

"Yeah, bro...the Aryan one...blonde hair, blue eyes...you know the one."

"Ah-Hahaha," I cracked up. "That is terrifying."

"He won't leave me alone, bro. I was looking through these giant books of art back there, trying to get my mind off him. But he was in every painting bro."

"Um Hmm. Oh God," I prompted, throwing some irony in for good measure.

"I tried walking around. Upstairs, in the movie section, downstairs in the kid's area...he keeps following me, always at a distance."

"Damn," I egged him on, "What's he doing now?"

"He's over by the low shelves where they keep the audiobooks. He's hiding behind the potted rubber plant near a Tony Robbins display."

"Holy shit," I laughed.

"I'm not laughing, Jay. This is fucking creepy, " he said, frantically.

I pictured Nick hiding in the alcove by the water fountains, peeking around the wall-papered corner.

"Are you seeing anything else?" I inquired.

"Turtles. There's turtles parachuting from the crystal chandeliers."

"Nice. Where are they going?"

"They are slowly walking across the carpet to the front door. From there it looks like they are rolling down the concrete steps. They're crawling over to the fountain, in the garden down there. They're swimming."

"Perfect," I said in a matter-of-fact tone. "Follow them. Go sit on one of the benches by the fountain. Listen to the water. Really listen to it."

"Okay, okay. I'm walking, I'm walking. Jesus is following."

"That's fine. He can follow. Just listen to the water."

"Okay, I'm on the bench. I'm listening."

"Okay, after I hang up, I want you to pick a tree, any tree on the edge of the courtyard. Stare past it, toward the sky, as long as you can without blinking."

"Stare past the tree. Got it."

"Yep. Stare past that tree and listen to the water until Red comes to pick you up."

"Gotcha. Thanks bro. I'm starting to feel better already."

"Yes you are. Peace, man."

"Peace."

leaves in the madhouse

Ultimately, the Lucy circus lasted about seven months, when all was said and done. The whole operation would have come crashing down sooner had it not been for the shape-shifting properties of the product.

The decision to close up shop stemmed from a few basic facts. The first, of course, was that distributors at the wholesale level were being questioned. The second fact was a subtle one, a gut feeling, that had been growing over time. I started to see what this product was doing to some kids - turning regular students into addicts with insatiable appetites, turning some into unrecognizable fiends. While I only used the product once a month (give or take), and very rarely in public, I soon realized that the appetites of many others had no check valve, nothing to prevent them from sliding down the slippery slope into the abyss.

The most vivid example of this excess came when my ex-girlfriend Maddie appeared, from out of the shadows, at a Halloween gathering. I was kicking back with a group of close friends. We were hanging out around a bonfire at Jaquie's house, having a few drinks. I hadn't seen Maddie since she was expelled from Waverly High.

Dew was already forming on the tips of grass blades. There was a giant leaf pile, into which some of us were jumping and wrestling. A few had taken Lucy for the occasion. Eerie jack-o-lanterns dotted the porch. A mutilated ventriloquist dummy sat on the porch, blood dripping from its mouth. Drinks graced our young palettes. Into this aire of spooky relaxation Maddie brought her addicted self back to my doorstep.

How had she tracked me down? She hopped out of the blue car, eyes large and manic, and ran over to me. The split ends of her disheveled hair wisped madly about her face. Catching sight of her, my gut tightened and I stood, bracing myself for her desperate, soul-sucking energy.

"Nope," I said.

"Pleeease, Jay, pleeease?" she pleaded insanely.

"Not today, Maddie... You have no handle on how much you're consuming. No self-control. You're done." I said, firmly.

"Pleease, Jay, pleease? I need more!"

Nick Scatterfield looked on at the scene, curiously. I held up a finger to him, as if to say, "Give me a sec."

"Maddie, I can't knowingly give you more when you're already at the edge. Do you have a deathwish? Step back from the edge, girl."

She began to scream and tug on my shirt. I wrenched it free from her grasp, tearing a sleeve at the seam. I motioned to her acquaintances, these fools who had driven her here.

"Get her out of here," I said. "She's embarrassing herself."

Each friend grabbed her under an arm, and started to drag her toward the car. She resisted wildly, at first clawing and kicking at them, and then going stiff, dragging gravel under her feet.

"We'll get her home," they assured me between gritted teeth.

The two wrestled her into the back seat of the car. I watched in the firelight, as she was driven off, pounding insanely on the back window with her fists. I had the impression she was being driven off to a mental ward. I looked up at the night sky, whose stars winked in the void. This had to stop, and soon...very soon.

Since she had successfully killed the mood, we decided to migrate in-doors, where someone turned on the *Rocky Horror Picture Show* and made popcorn. I had never seen this flick, and as I sat in a giant brown armchair stuffing popcorn kernels in my face, confusion grew. Maddie's desperate negativity, her bad vibes, still radiated through my frame as I watched a transvestite in black leather parade across the screen. They broke into song, and began to move seductively across the stage. I had no conceptual framework for this type of entertainment, and my faltering thoughts began to pile up. Cognitive dissonance. Paranoia seeped in. Chaos loomed.

Jaquie's parents walked in the door not long afterward, and I recoiled even further into my solitaire paranoiac silence. Thankfully, Nick and Red Scatterfield were engaged in conversation with her parents, and we ended up leaving soon after that. Too much sensory input for my reeling senses.

When I returned home from the party, I flushed all that remained of my Lucy supply. This wrinkle in time was coming to a close. I watched as it swirled in the aquamarine water of the toilet bowl. I cut all ties with sellers and suppliers. When anyone asked what had happened to the source, I just muttered something vague about it drying up. I shuffled my feet across the linoleum floors of the school, which now seemed somehow transformed, forever altered by the scenes of the last seven months.

About a week after my decision to close up shop, I noticed tinted-out, black unmarked cars patrolling the country roads near my house. This only further confirmed for me that I had made the right decision. I felt a palpable weight lift from my shoulders. The paranoia and suspicion began to dissipate. Operation Lucy had been shelved. The moment had passed. Waverly had nudged me further toward the gates of hell, but through some gut-level intuition, some conscience, some inner voice, I had pivoted. I found myself eating my ego, rather than ego tripping, at the gates of hell. Unlike Mr. Petty, I felt that backing down at the gates of hell was the only moral option at that point. I couldn't lie to myself any longer.

Side effects of Lucy include the following:

The ability to make sensible judgments and see common dangers is impaired. A user might try to step out a window to get a "closer look" at the ground. He might consider it fun to admire the sunset, blissfully unaware that he is standing in the middle of a busy intersection.

Many users experience flashbacks, or a recurrence of the trip, often without warning, long after taking.

Bad trips and flashbacks are only part of the risks of use. Users may manifest relatively long-lasting psychoses or severe depression.

Because the substance accumulates in the body, users develop a tolerance for the drug. In other words, some repeat users have to take it in increasingly higher doses to achieve a "high." This increases the physical effects and also the risk of a bad trip that could cause psychosis.

Source: Foundation for a Drug-Free World

norm's countenance

Our clique moved fluidly through the murky waters of Waverly's anarchistic, hedonistic subculture, a social cell performing its proper function - testing and retesting the limits of her patience. Our physical safety and security rested upon the somewhat straight-laced efforts of our parents, as they worked diligently to shore up Waverly's norm.

Middle class salaries and working class cash purchased our freedom to indulge in bouts of disorderly conduct. Occasionally, serious, unintended consequences reminded us how thinly we were insulated from being consumed, how quickly our little worlds could crumble at a moment's notice. The death of Norm was such an event.

Let me backup for a minute…

We were typically an inclusive group of freethinkers, expanding and contracting our circle across many other social cells, creating a sort of symbiosis. We bonded over any number of things: compulsory education, unrealistic expectations, relationships, music, substances...life in general. Our clique was a Millennial Breakfast Club. Because of this tendency toward inclusion, rather than exclusion, it was all-the-more notable for an extreme event to disrupt the balance. But Waverly had her whims, which she insisted we entertain...

Norm was a closed book to us, a classmate in Leming's gym class where Nick Scatterfield, Tre Moreno and I either skipped out to smoke or started up hacky-sack circles in defiance of Leming's instructions. Norm sometimes emerged from the sidelines to join the circle, hiking up his baggy pants to catch the hemp sack in the crook of his Airwalk skate shoe. I recall the skinny black-haired boy who laughed hysterically, hopping from foot to foot as he juggled the bead-filled sack. Norm even had a signature move where he would sandwich the hacky sack between his two navy-colored skate shoes and do a handstand, simultaneously flinging the sack across the circle with his feet. It was always a good day when Norm joined the circle.

Leming was a birdlike man, stick legs with a bulging torso, small head with glasses perched precariously on the skinny bridge of his nose. Following one period of our typical hacky sack insubordination, Leming was fuming. I sensed the steam rising from his feathery hair. Brow furrowed in consternation, he motioned me over to his office, along one side of the gym, near the boys locker room. He sat on the edge of his desk facing me.

He accused me of being the "ringleader" of the group, encouraging others to follow suit and opt out of gym class. When I opened my mouth to speak, he shut me down. He continued to bark threats and allegations at me for five minutes straight, only relenting when he looked at the clock. Most of Leming's pet students were already changed and waiting in line for the bell to ring. I marched out past them, returning to the locker room in such a rage that I impulsively kicked the drinking fountain off the wall, flooding the locker room with our signature brand of antic hay. Norm's small face peered around the corner, wide-eyed and open-mouthed, at first. Then he began to cackle maniacally.

Leming flung open the double doors and scampered in to find a group of us half-dressed, staring at the gushing pipeline. The metal fountain lay in disarray on the floor.

"Who's responsible for this?" Leming demanded.

"Damn thing just fell off the wall," Norm offered in a dumbfounded tone, "craziest shit I've ever seen."

"I've never seen anything quite like that either," I offered too, innocently.

Leming went ballistic.

"I know it was you Chapparal!" he spat.

"There you go again, throwing out accusations like candy to kids on Halloween. Trick or treat, Leming, trick or treat."

He cursed all of us and stormed out to hyena laughter. Nothing ever came of it.

One day, late in the school year, we took the antics too far in Leming's class. The period ended uneventfully, and Moreno came to me, in a rare, hyped mood, itching to fuck with someone. Norm had a stash of weed in his bag, Moreno said. The backpack was hanging in the boys' locker room. He thought it would be funny for one of us to distract Norm, while the other grabbed his leafy greens. Without a second thought, I agreed, as I generally did with Moreno's schemes, and as he typically did with mine. We were always fucking with each other just to entertain ourselves, if nothing else.

If I recall correctly, Moreno faked a little scuffle with Norm, in order to distract him, hopping around him throwing fake punches like a prize fighter in a ring. Meanwhile, I, in the process of changing back into my street clothes, smoothly executed the grab-and-go. Norm and Moreno rounded the corner, both a little tousled, as I picked up my book bag and headed out of the locker room, a newly acquired sandwich baggie of buds nestled deep in my right hand pocket.

Norm quickly figured that one of us had copped his stash, or that Leming had confiscated it. Of course, he couldn't report any of this to the principals. I'm not sure if we smoked the stuff, or intended to just hold onto it for a bit to make him sweat. Either way, the fallout was far beyond what we intended.

Evidently that sandwich bag of sunshine was the only thing keeping Norm from slipping off into the abyss.

When we arrived at school the next morning, we began to hear whispers that Norm had blown his face off. The really terrible thing was that Norm didn't even get suicide 'right,' if such a thing can be said for such a desperate and hopeless act. He had aimed the long barrel at the wrong angle and shearing his damn face off, prompting his parents to discover him a bloody, writhing mess in their barn. Terrible screams issued from that hellish hole where their boy's face had recently been. He passed away shortly after, from blood loss, the hay and dry earth drinking up the vital forces from Norm's veins. An unnatural silence fills that barn to this day.

I went back and forth for a long time on whether or not to include this episode in my tales. It weighs heavily on Scatterfield, Moreno and I to this day. The three of us met up and discussed the event years later, each of us growing somber and shaking our heads in residual confusion.

"I think about that kid..." Moreno offered.

"It was just so unlike us to do something like that. What do you think came over us?" I pondered.

"We broke every unspoken rule of herb culture that day," Moreno noted, baffled.

"If I could take one thing back, that'd be it." I noted decisively.

"Same." Moreno agreed.

"Yeah, but you guys can't be responsible for Norm's actions," Nick countered. "There's no way you could've known what kind of demons Norm was dealing with."

"I know you're right, bro. I just wish I hadn't piled weight on a sinking ship." I massaged my temples, trying for clarity.

"I hear you, man, but what's done is done. You sure as hell can't bring him back. And I don't know that he'd want to be brought back if you could." Nick concluded, ever the one to offer a counterpoint.

I finally decided to include this dark episode out of respect for you, reader. I would not be honest with you if I didn't admit that our reckless behavior occasionally had regrettable, unintended consequences.

At one point, I thought I might be able to imagine what Norm might have been going through, what would force him to take such drastic measures. I went to bed that night attempting to empathize, to visualize a mind in the throes of such desperation. That night I had one of the worst nightmares I've ever had. A dark wind howled into my ears, and all my limbs were tied. An inky, oily blackness poured over me, practically suffocating me. I wracked my brain for a way out of this cyclone pinning me down, this force which seemed intent on tugging my soul from my body. Through the howling wind, I heard a small voice reminding me to pray. I did so, commanding the force to release me in the manner I had been taught. I felt myself yanked out from the darkness, and awoke in a tangled mess of sweaty sheets. As my frantic breath slowed, I somehow knew, very clearly, that I would never ever be able to imagine what such a tortured soul must feel. I thanked God for the clarity of the thought and then attempted to live a normal day of normal life.

Out of all the crazy shit we pulled, messing with Norm is by far the one that Moreno and I regret the most. This act snipped the last thread from which he dangled over the flames of hell. On the one hand, Moreno and I can't be accountable for someone's drastic decision to end their life. On the other hand, we can be accountable for not supporting a comrade in his path through the wasteland of Waverly. The episode runs so counter to our typical modus operandi that it baffles us to this day. Were we not in possession of ourselves that day? What demons had we welcomed? We should have pulled him up with us, rather than letting him fall. It is easy to connect the dots looking backward, but we couldn't have known...We had lost another to the cruel hand of Waverly. But we couldn't help feeling that we had killed the Norm.

snakes in the grass

While I had called it quits on selling Lucy, Waverly's finest had not called it quits on getting to the source of Lucy. I was to witness a series of even more unfortunate events, not unlike those described by Mr. Snicket in his catalogue of tales.

One overcast morning at Waverly High, I was drinking a screwdriver near my locker, swishing the orange juice and vodka across my tongue before swallowing it down. Savoring the swirl of flavors, I was staring off across the hall, lost in thought.

Sam ran up to me, out of breath, her tie-dyed deady bear t-shirt clinging to her lanky chest.

"They got Moreno," Sam huffed, trying to catch her breath.

"What do you mean? Who got Moreno?" I prompted, throwing my bottle in the locker and slamming it shut.

"Admin," she said. "They hired an undercover cop to enroll as a student. He got Moreno, Jay."

I took a minute to process, reflectively.

"Who was it - the snake? Do we have a name? His legal name?"

"Daniel Crumpkin," Sam breathed, finally calming a little, brushing her disheveled hair out of her eyes.

"I need a photo," I said. "Get me an image, quick, fast, and in a hurry. Meet me near the Media Center."

I headed in one direction to spread the news and assemble a team. Sam lurched off in the other direction. Within about ten minutes, Sam was passing off a snapshot of the undercover officer to me in front of the Media Center.

My small entourage headed straight into the Library, over to a row of desktop computers near the copiers and printers. Within fifteen minutes we had more basic info on the cop. Within 30 minutes, the library copiers were running full force, spitting out fliers with the name, picture, and likely whereabouts of the snake. I grabbed a stack, hot off the copier, and shoved it into the waiting hands of a team member.

"Get going. Post them on walls. Pass them out."

I awaited more stacks to issue from the copiers, passing them off to other team members. In this way the fliers hit the walls of the halls, the bulletin boards, and the hands of students. We distributed them at the height of lunchhour in the packed cafeteria. Someone began emailing the info to friends at other schools. We were young and dumb, but we were crowdsourcing before the days of social media. We were fighting back against a soul-sucking creature, a system that was chewing up our friends as we spoke. I wasn't sure how successful our efforts would be, but I couldn't just sit on my ass while brothers got shackled. We were casting stones at a colossal presence.

I was disgusted when I finally got the entire news story. All the nearby counties had created a "drug task force." One of the main "tasks" they were given was to rid the schools of "drugs." The force unleashed undercover drug investigators into all the nearby schools.

Crumpkin, an unassuming 20-something with long brown hair, met Moreno through our mutual friend Crystal. We were all veterans of the Pinehouse Grille, and had gotten even closer after Jared peaced out. After Jared caught a mouthful of cornfield, Crystal had begun to smoke more. Moreno usually hooked Crystal up with buds, at cost, out of respect for Jared.

The student cop had gradually inserted himself into the flow of Waverly High before he started asking if anyone knew where he could score some weed or other substances. His locker was nearby Crystal's and she, being a sweet person, quickly befriended him. Crumpkin wasn't overly insistent, but gradually began mentioning how he wouldn't mind scoring some smoke or a few pills if she knew of anyone who could come through. He explained to her that since he was new to the area, he needed some new hook-ups. Crystal eventually mentioned it to Tre Moreno. Tre, being a nice dude, agreed to meet up with the guy outside of school to sell him a sack.

At that time, Moreno had long dark hair, wore baggy jeans, and loose fitting Doors t-shirts. Other than being a stoner, Moreno had one more strike against him: he was Mexican in a predominantly "white" middle class school. Am I saying he was racially profiled? Well, yes. Yes I am.

The administration, working with Crumpkin and the drug task force, lured Moreno into a "school zone." within so many yards of a neighborhood elementary school, and nabbed him there. Crumpkin couldn't get Moreno to bring weed to Waverly High, so they executed the entrapment elsewhere.

In Indiana, in those days, selling weed in "a drug-free zone" or "school zone" carried with it a mandatory minimum felony sentence with two years jailtime. Moreno got exactly that - a felony and time for helping a random guy get a bag of herb. It's no wonder that folks have trust issues and paranoia accompanies drug use in backwater states like Indiana.

Pinned down by that F-word, jobs would be hard to come by once Moreno saw the light of day again. He was smacked down by a white hand in a white land. Terrorized for not living by the moral norm. I was in a state of utter shock, lured into Waverly by that shy and easy-going smile, only to see her fangs in full force, at the necks of my friends. The contrast was disturbing.

Crystal and Moreno began to date while he was behind bars. She started to visit him regularly, bringing him news from the outside. In those days, he lived vicariously through her. She would twirl her sandy hair at the visitation booth and lean toward the glass, describing future plans, in which they overcame all odds. I really think she kept him alive while he was locked in Waverly's basement.

They eventually did overcome the social stigma of criminal conviction, after years upon years of fighting to have his record expunged. I think it took a decade. They moved away from Waverly's hungry eyes and had a few kids. Ironically, marijuana is now legal in most states, at some level. But the collateral damage from the War on Drugs is still lurking below the surface, it's ripples still flowing across the land. Victims still sit in Waverly's basement.

I would like to report that the pressure we exerted gave Crumpkin no choice but to leave the area, flee the state. That would be at least one small victory in the battle of our youth. I used to imagine street justice coming his way. But in all likelihood, Crumpkin was lauded for his work in weeding out the "bad apples" and was transferred to another school where he continued construction of the school-to-jail pipeline.

After Moreno's arrest, the local paper printed a front page interview with the principal, where he spoke about the undercover efforts to rid the school of drugs. He called operation WASP a glowing success, explaining how they had netted the big fish in the school. He assured the public that no other fish like this existed or could exist in the school. What a fucking PR stunt. If it hadn't been for Moreno, I would have laughed out loud when I saw it. Sticking with his metaphor, the "task force" comes in for a month, skims off some little fish with their minnow nets, and spin it as a successful fishing trip. They netted no Lucy, no opiates, no methamphetamines. Just a few unsuspecting potheads. What a fucking witch hunt, it was...

I might not have had the vocabulary for it at the time, but now I see quite clearly that whenever there is a dominant oppressive culture, there is an equally pervasive counterculture below the surface. For every action, there is an equal and opposite reaction…Unfortunately, the counterculture often feeds the Fear Factory of the dominant culture which allows them further justification for Waverly to wrap her reptilian arms around us.

pharma bums

One rainy evening, I sat bathed in black light, rocking gently in my favorite wicker chair. I stared off into space, across the purple light, contemplating Prodigy's lyrics which cut through my speakers: "Take a picture! Slap my chick up!" The hypnotic electronic beats flowed through my subwoofers, pulsing out across my room. *This guy has some fucking issues*, I thought to myself. My mom stomped on the floor, signaling that my music was too loud. I adjusted the volume slightly, and heard her heavy footfall recede toward the other end of the house.

As the thunder rumbled across the sky, my stomach began to rumble below. I rose, walked across the textured area rug. I opened the hardwood, six panel door that closed off my space from the rest of the vast basement. In anticipation, my mind shuffled through snack options. I began to climb the wide hardwood stairs that led to the main floor of my parents' house, up from my drywall cave.

I heard my mother speaking in hushed tones to my father, probably across the butcher block island in the kitchen. The house was surprisingly quiet for a weeknight. Something different about my mother's tone made me stop halfway up the stairs. I sat down on a brightly lacquered oak step, tracing the wood grain with my fingers.

In those days, my mother worked as a nurse, and had just come home from her four-hour evening shift. I visualized her standing at the island in her scrubs, leafing through the day's mail, splitting a beer with my dad, as she often did on particularly stressful days. I felt awkward, eavesdropping on my parents, but something in her tone fastened me to the spot.

"It's not right,Tom," she was saying.

I could picture my dad nodding in concern, brow furrowed.

"These poor people come into the clinic. They're haggard-looking, shaky, and obviously strung out. They tell the receptionist what they 'need' and Dr. Stevens writes the prescription - no questions asked."

"Have you said anything?" My dad asked.

I could picture him coming around to rub my mother's shoulders, in an effort to comfort her worried mind.

"Oh no, I don't want to get in the middle of it. I don't think it's my place. Not to mention, if the place does get shut down, I don't want Dr. Stevens to think I was the one who reported them. He's a nice man. Just too nice."

Silence hovered for a minute. In my mind's eye, I saw my father churning the news over, running calculations, rubbing his clean-shaven chin with his right hand.

"You'll have to give them your two-week notice, find something else. We'll make it work."

"Do you think I should submit the notice as soon as tomorrow, Tom?"

"The sooner, the better," he said decisively.

I rose slowly, and tip-toed back down the stairs in my socks, my belly still rumbling for an evening snack. I knew that tone. When my father had that tone, the discussion was over. Not long after that, my mother was working a new job, as a nurse at a regional walk-in clinic. I think her nerves were sufficiently calmed by the change in employers. But that didn't solve the underlying issue. Who were these haggard adults? I wondered. From under which crevice did they crawl? Back in my room, I sat down and pondered this for a bit, feeling even better about my decision to quit selling Lucy.

As I've mentioned, I wasn't a pill-popper, even at the height of my anarchistic revels. In my circle, pills had a bad connotation, a shadowy stigma attached to them. Moreno was the only one I knew that sometimes popped a few pills. I did also know a few kids that had started taking pills from parents, or buying them on the street - maybe even from those folks Dr. Stevens supplied.

And then, there was the kid down the street who had overdosed on Morphine, and was currently in a treatment center. There was that new Asian kid, we called The Goat. Word was that he was The Pill Guy at Waverly High.

What would become of this pill charade my mom mentioned? I wondered. Would this call for further clamp-downs by the drug task force? Who would break the cycle? My stomach rumbled again, disrupting my thoughts. I shut my door noisily, and stomped across the basement to give warning of my approach.

"Mom?" I shouted, "Do we have any cereal left?"

"Come look in the pantry, Jay," she cooed, slightly raising her voice. "I'm not your personal inventory manager."

I smiled to myself, and went up to grab a bowl of Golden Grahams and milk.

Not long after overhearing that conversation, I got to know the Goat a little better. I ran into him at the Scatterfield place, and smoked with him a few times as we wove through the backroads of Waverly in his bright red Honda CRX. His given name was Jian Shanyang, and he had just moved to the area from Detroit. Several times, he offered a few pills to me, but I politely declined. The

Goat lived in a small Waverly apartment with his single mom, who worked two jobs just to get by. Needless to say, he had very little oversight, and a lot of time on his hands.

At one point, a few months after we had been formally introduced, I stopped by his place to drop off a bag of herb. I walked up the concrete and wrought iron stairs to the second floor apartment. I knocked three times. Through the stormdoor, he called for me to come right in. I figured he was engrossed in the video game he was usually playing. I tugged on the cheap stormdoor and its unoiled hinges creaked open. The scent of incense wafted to me. I heard voices coming from a back bedroom. I made my way toward the voices, across the shaggy blue carpet.

When I crossed the threshold, the ghostly form of Waverly was draped across the Goat's lap. The back of her Blind Melon t-shirt scrunched up as she twisted around to inspect me. Staring out from the shirt was a little girl dressed as a bee. The bee girl's face twisted, as if in pain as Waverly contorted her upper body.

"Hey Jay," she said, in her whimsical, airy kind of way.

"Thanks for bringing us some bud."

She flashed me a sinister, sexy look. Her eyes were bloodshot, and drool hovered at the edge of her large lips. The Goat had a lazy, sedated look on his face.

"The caaash issss on the dresser, bro."

I took a step toward the dresser and snatched up the fifty dollar bill, from under an ashtray, tossing the baggie on top of the dresser. Waverly directed her attention back to the Goat, grabbing his chin with her right hand and turning his head to face her. She grabbed his dark hair violently, forcing him to stare at her. A hand went up into her shirt, and withdrew a transparent orange bottle with a white cap. Locking eyes with the Goat, she pushed down and twisted on the cap. I felt a vague, gnawing nervousness in my stomach. I sensed something heavy, oppressive, and suddenly felt very out of place.

"I'll leave you guys to it," I said awkwardly, backing toward the door.

"Thanks, Jay," Waverly whispered, waving backward, over her shoulder.

She was wiggling a large pill between the Goat's closed lips as I left. The Goat flashed me a tranquil smile and waved as I threw up a reluctant peace sign.

"Deuces," he said groggily.

I jogged back across the blue carpet, and out the stormdoor. The brisk chill of the grey Indiana afternoon assaulted my nostrils. As I walked down the sidewalk, I watched the orange and yellow leaves fall from the giant row of maples and oaks that lined the road. The crisp autumn air rejuvenated my thoughts, made me pensive, but hopeful.

Later that afternoon, I got a call from Nick Scatterfield.

"Hey brother, just wanted to let you know that they found the Goat unresponsive a few hours ago. Some sort of horse tranquilizer in his system. They weren't able to resuscitate."

I looked out the window and heaved a heavy sigh, watching the passing clouds. I was silent. It seemed my life was steadily becoming a bridge of sighs.

"You still there?" Nick asked.

"Yeah, yeah. I'm here... That's fucking depressing, man."

"I just can't see any other way it could have ended. Those tranqs are some serious shit bro..." Scatterfield offered stoically.

The Goat's funeral was on a Saturday. I didn't go. I had chores to do, and I didn't want my family to think I was wrapped up in that shit.

shake a leg

After three tragic deaths and a brother locked down in the system, I was incredibly ready to kick back and kill a few brain cells. I felt Waverly closing in on me and I needed to pull myself together.

Red Scatterfield and I were lounging at my pad in the wicker furniture my grandparents had given me when they had updated their "sunroom" furnishings. Red brought Danilo Montanez, a kid I had partied with before out at the Ranch. We rocked relaxedly back and forth, Danilo in the grey chair, I in the white. Red sat in a pleather beanbag chair nearby.

We each had a drink in hand. Gin and juice was a favorite in those days, in honor of Snoop. Classic rock tunes poured from the surround sound speakers mounted around the walkout basement bedroom. Aerosmith's "Walk This Way" assaulted us. We had just returned from smoking, out among the mowed paths of my parents' property.

Fifteen-year-old Danilo had a side hustle, selling stereo equipment at wholesale prices. Red had introduced me to Danilo and, with some of the accumulated proceeds from Lucy, I had recently purchased a state-of-the-art sound system for my room, through him. I was in the process of ordering one for my future ride as well, if my parents ever let me own a vehicle. Both Danilo and I shared this entrepreneurial bent, which was actively discouraged at Waverly High.

We sat back and shot the shit over our gin drinks, to the sound of Steven Tyler's crooning. I owned no TV in those days. Neither did my parents. It was a long-held belief in my family that TV turned people into idiots. The "boob tube," they called it. There was an oft recounted story in my family of the day when my mom's father had returned home from a long day at the law office, only to find six of his seven kids so fixated on the television that they were unresponsive to his conversational questions or verbal demands.

He marched over and unlatched the living room window, flinging it open. As he yanked the TV from its pedestal, the plug pulled free of its socket, the picture disappearing. With great effort, he heaved it down into the ravine below. (Evidently televisions were incredibly heavy in those days.) My aunts and uncles, the spell broken, ran over to the window in time to see the bouncing box finish its descent. What was left of it came to rest against a tree. A gaping hole, where the screen had been, glared up at them from its bed of fallen leaves. They stared up at my Grandpa, uncomprehendingly. There has been no television ever since. I say all this to make the point that music was our sweet surrender.

As Red, Danilo, and I veered from one topic to the next, Danilo suddenly sat up, wide-eyed. I stopped rocking and stared at him, thinking he had heard something I didn't, or he just remembered he had to be somewhere. Quick as lightning, Danilo tugged off his left leg, and hurled it at my face.

"Think fast!" he shouted.

Impulsively, I ducked, and the leg landed with a thud on the coffee table beside me, the boot hanging off the side. Somehow, I had managed not to spill my grape juice and gin, which sloshed from side to side in my glass. My eyes fixated on the vestigial leg which now lay beside me on the small wooden table. My mouth hung open in shock as my eyes darted from the leg to Danilo to Red, from Red to Danilo to the leg. Finally, a giant smirk appeared on their faces.

"It's a prosthetic, Jay," Red laughed.

"What the hell?" I finally managed, relieved laughter starting to rock the three of us.

I picked up the inanimate leg and tossed it back to him. I thought back. I visualized him as he walked down the wide hallways of the school, a slight limp in his gait. I never thought anything of it. Ahh, I thought. Again, hindsight was 20/20.

Still my mind reeled. I saw this kid off and on for over a year now, and I hadn't noticed his false leg? Truly nothing was what it seemed. As we went back to sipping on our drinks, he settled his leg back in its place and told me the story.

"A while back, I went deer hunting with some friends," Danilo began, leaning forward and rubbing his palms together.

"We went out in the evening, just before dark. There's a stand of trees over by my dad's place, on the edge of a cornfield. It's a nice spot, with a tree stand and all…We had our shotguns with us. It was only my second or third time going. I was the first one to the ladder, so, with gun in hand, I began to awkwardly climb the ladder up to the tree stand. The wooden ladder rungs were a bit slick with moss. One of the other guys said something from below. I turned around to look down at them. In the process, my shotgun slipped from my fingers, and hit the ground, firing up in my direction. The blast hit my leg, but somehow missed anything vital. Somehow the safety got switched off during my climb. What are the chances?"

"Holy shit!" I said, leaning forward, hungry for the details.

Danilo nodded, dramatically.

"Shot me right in the left leg. Of course I fell from the ladder down into the leaves. It all happened so fast...There was blood everywhere, all over the tree, the ladder, and the leaves. I laid on my back and looked up at the sky through the remaining leaves above. I've never been in so much pain, Jay. At some point I passed out. The guys thought quickly. They tied my leg off so I didn't bleed out. They got me up between them and somehow managed me back to my dad's place, across the cornfields. Someone called an ambulance, which arrived soon after."

When Danilo finished, Red and I sat staring at him across from us. We never know what someone's been through unless we ask. I think at that point, I started allowing for the possibility that everyone had been through some crazy shit. I just had to dig a little deeper to unearth it.

a trip to the mushroom planet

One summer night, Nick Scatterfield and I decided to take a mushroom trip. We had tried many things together over the years, and while we were hedonists in those days, we did have our limits, though these limits may seem ridiculous and random to most. As I've mentioned, we weren't "pill-poppers". At its root, our brand of hedonism was of the natural sort: adrenaline, ale, and herb. I had made an exception to this rule during the Lucy craze. Nick's exception was ecstasy, another popular drug at the time, whereas, I wouldn't touch the stuff. Too unpredictable, I thought. Acid was psychological, whereas ecstasy was emotional. Plus, I'd heard the stories of kids dying at raves due to dehydration and other side effects of ecstasy. We had decided to try "shrooms" because we heard they were essentially nature's version of Lucy. I think Nick may have tried them before, but it was my first time.

I chipped in, and Nick purchased the quarter-ounce bag of mushroom caps. We decided to head to the Mount Comfort mall and see what was going down. We grabbed a pizza in the food court, found a table in the middle of the crowded space, and I watched as Nick's pale hand added this psychedelic seasoning to the cheese pizza. The bitter caps needed a little help on the flavor front, when it came to ingesting them.

We sat and chatted as we consumed slice after slice of the somewhat greasy evening meal. People floated this way and that, criss-crossing in their paths to alternate destinations. The tropical plants were perched sporadically throughout the spaces, listening to the buzz of conversation and that generic mall music. The tunes seemed to prime shoppers to feel that all was right with the world, as they filled their bags with the colorful nothings from sweatshops in foreign lands. Ads and billboards lured people into stores, promising comfort, or style, or sex appeal.

We finished the meal, tossed the pizza box, and got up to stroll through the vast waxed corridors of this consumer paradise. We nodded at the chubby mall cop as he passed. He was making his rounds, keeping the Mount Comfort mall safe for consumption. I saw no recognition in his eyes. Nick and I's shoplifting spree had been years prior, and thousands of faces flowed past the eyes of that unfortunate mall cop every day. Our teen heads bobbed through the crowd, my shaggy brown dreads and Nick's more noticeable blonde mop. We sipped on some juices and continued to stroll and people-watch.

We turned a corner and came upon Spencer's. We swerved over to enter the store, which was awash with purplish black light. A girl with dark lipstick and a spiked dog collar glared at me as I entered. If she was mad at the world, she definitely wasn't upping her odds with the bitchface and the outfit. Or maybe she was hired as the guard dog? The costume companies were really capitalizing on the "goth" movement in those days. The general look could be described as sado-masochistic heroin addict chic. I bought into the craze a bit myself, following bands like the Voodoo Glow Skulls and Rancid.

I started leafing through posters in the oversized display which fanned out from the side wall. Scatterfield wandered further back, checking out the gag gifts and other eccentric items they stocked. My fingers continued flipping through the steel poster frames. I paused at a blacklight poster that was done up in fluorescent oranges, yellows, and greens. It was a wizard, standing by a hut with his walking stick. He gazed out from the poster with penetrating eyes. Fluorescent waves emanated from him. I let myself be drawn into the art, entranced. The waves which rippled out from this cloaked figure gradually morphed into a clear tunnel around me. A tingling sensation washed over my body. The trip was on. I was "tripping balls," as we said in those days. Perhaps we put it that way because it felt as if the spirit of the Trip itself grabbed us by the genitals and catapulted us into some unseen psychedelic dimension. I called Nick over, and we stared into the fluorescent world of the wizard for a bit longer. After a time, we wandered back out of the store, into the artificial daylight of the larger shopping experience.

There was a commotion off to our left. The fountain in the commons area overflowed with bubbles. Frothy foam spilled over on all sides, washing over the concrete sides as kids laughed with glee. Teens chuckled to themselves, parents shook their heads in dismay, and the mall cops looked on in general disbelief, scratching their heads. Nick and I burst out laughing at the sight of this unexpected scene. Bubbles wafted on the breeze. Under the spell of the shrooms, we saw not only the mountains of bubbles, but the echoes of those bubbles as they popped. There was a loud crinkle to them, which issued rippling purple vibrations in all directions. I watched those pops rickashay off the plastered beige walls, and the glass ceiling above the fountain. Colorful conversations hovered in the air around the spewing, frothy fountain. The mall cops radioed maintenance, asking for the fountain to be turned off. A few minutes later, from within the esoteric chambers behind the visible walls, came a hunched woman with a giant metal ring of keys. The janitor hobbled over to a grey panel. She opened it, found the right key, inserted, and turned. The bubbles immediately stopped, beginning to recede and implode upon themselves. We looked on open-mouthed as they began dissolving magically into the night. The show was over. The other bystanders started to trickle away. We did so as well.

Our trip was only beginning. Nick and I headed toward the north exit to meet my mom and my little cousin Adeline, who had been elsewhere, shopping. The summer night air was warm with purpose. The pheromones of the season wafted into my flared nostrils. We stepped up to the edge of the concrete curb, and waited as my mom's white Honda pulled up to the curb. Addie's excited young face filled the passenger side window. Nick and I filed into the tan, cushioned back seat. Generalities were exchanged. Nick thanked my mom for the ride. He was always super polite to my parents, who he vaguely sensed hated him for unknown reasons. I had tried telling him that this wasn't the case. They were just super uptight and strict, because in trying to parent us, they were navigating a reality about which they knew nothing.

My mom artfully swerved in and out of traffic down Columbus Boulevard, making her way toward the interstate, which would float the vehicle north, past Waverly, out to my parents' house in the hills. I was trip-dizzy, wrapped up in a glowing, but translucent cocoon, serrated with bluish-purple edges and archs. Nick and I gazed out our respective windows into the darkness of the night. Cars, trucks, and eighteen wheelers sped by, leaving red and yellow tracers as they passed, blurred lines of what had been, only a moment before, like a beautiful watercolor painting. I often wondered what my parents thought, if they ever noticed me in the process of contemplating these other worlds. My mom reached over and pushed a black plastic button on the dash. Simon and Garfunkel began singing their poetry into my trip.

Visual echoes from the cymbal crashes floated as pink lines in front of me. Lyrics from "The Boxer" bobbed and bounced through my mental space, turning in on themselves. I floated along, over the interstate, in this private psychedelic concert.

Paul and Art broke through again, shifting moods. Little Addie brushed her long hair behind her ear.

"Why do you think he would rather be a sparrow than a snail, Auntie?"

Nick gave me a surprised look, which set me to giggling.

"Good question. I don't know, Addie," my mom responded, absent-mindedly.

It was a great question. The reeling cogs of my mind creaked along, and began to contemplate the relative merits of sparrowdom vs snaildom. Soaring heights would be the obvious choice...the protective shell of the snail, though... the flighty, darting presence of the sparrow...the slow methodical movement of the snail... The moments began to pull and stretch out, as the borders of mental space dissolved. The harmonic duo sang on.

Hmm, I thought...hammer or nail? ...the force from above, or the piece of steel that binds two things together? Impulsively, I'd pick the hammer. I saw the arch of its swing as it connected with the nail, spraying sparks...but the more I thought about it, the nail seemed more valuable...binding together, making two separate pieces one larger structure....although both are necessary for the process to work... So went my thoughts as we tripped on down the summer darkness of the interstate.

I was somehow surprised when we arrived at my parents' place, the towering, tan structure that had risen out of the earth at my father's command. Floodlights peered out from every corner, turning darkness into daylight. My mom and Addie went inside to begin nightime routines. Nick and I walked around back to start a bonfire on the flat section of lawn near the downstairs door to the walk-out basement. We were still rolling pretty hard, on down that strange trip through the mushroom planet. Sounds became sights. Thoughts took on physical form. We got the fire roaring and sat gazing into the twisting, curling, writhing flames. The backyard floodlights went to sleep for the night, setting the stage for a nocturnal rite. The glowing, shifting embers began to congregate toward the heart of the pile. Orange shapes and forms flew at us, out from this flaming eye in the heart of the darkness. A pillar of smoke unfolded, stretching itself into the upper world, as far as I could see. Small glowing figures darted up the pillar, never to be seen again.

At some point I volunteered to go inside to grab some drinks and snacks. I'm not sure how long I was gone, but when I stepped back out into the firelit darkness, Nick was reeling hard. With a worried expression, Nick told me that he saw my mom, leaning out the dining room window, scolding him for a range of imagined infractions. I told him that couldn't be the case since I had been up in the kitchen, which was just off the dining room. I would have noticed such a scene. At any rate, that wasn't something my mom would ever do. She would have spoken with me, and had me pass a message on to Nick, if she wanted to communicate something to him. Nick seemed to accept my explanation, but he brooded for a bit. We consumed whatever snacks I had procured...sandwiches or chips, or something of the sort. We continued our gaze into the raging pit.

"Did I mention the giant shadow-rabbit I saw?" Nick asked, breaking the silence. "It hopped up to the fire and sat for a few minutes, warming its large shadowy nose, and then scampered off over there." He gestured off into the darkness.

I gazed across the smoke at him as he told me the story. A smirk spread on my face.

"You're going pretty hard, brother. The darkness really did a number on your trip."

He looked around, like he expected someone to be listening.

"You want to go inside man?" I asked. He nodded his head, affirmatively.

We lounged in my blacklit room, wicker chairs rocking under us, listening to some tunes. Nick picked up a pencil and started sketching in a sketchpad he found laying on my table. The sounds of the summer night flowed through the open window. My mind's eye stared off into mental space, digesting the worlds opened to me through the lyrics of the song and the lens of the mushrooms. The physical world fell away from me, while Nick continued to sketch shapes and faces, and other miscellania that revealed themselves to him. At some point, I started to come down to Earth. I entered a sleepy phase of the trip. While I continued to hallucinate, I grew tired, and flopped on my unmade bed.

Psychedelic dreams spun in my head, fluorescent signs and symbols, images from unknown origins. Still, Nick feverishly sketched, pausing occasionally to stare off into space.

At some point, I awoke to Nick shaking my arm.

"Jay, wake up."

I sat upright, rubbing my eyes. I looked up at Nick who paced nearby, his blonde hair disheveled.

"I don't know how, Jay, I don't know how, but the government just did an experiment on my head."

He said it so matter-of-factly that it took me a moment to process.

"Huh?" I finally managed… "What do you mean 'did an experiment on your head?'"

Nick sat down, rubbing his brow.

"I don't know how, but I felt it Jay, I felt them running the experiment."

I stared at him in disbelief, a vague sense of dread washing over me. I still felt the effects of the mushrooms, though to a lesser, sleepier extent. His comments made so little sense that they threw my mind into a panic. I was suddenly a search engine with search criteria that wouldn't compute. I stared at him searchingly, panicked thoughts continuing to pour up from an unknown source. *Dammit*, I thought to myself, *I was having a good trip. Why'd you have to go and say some crazy shit like that?* Finally I managed to say something outloud:

"That's fucking crazy, man. You going to be alright?"

Nick looked up at me, and then off into space again.

"I don't know, man. I don't know. I'm not so sure."

I eyed him warily for a moment.

"Hmm," I mused. "Let's talk about this shit tomorrow when the sun is up. Maybe you'll feel better."

I hated this feeling of dread and panic. With my mind racing, I vowed that I would never do mushrooms again. On a gut level, I sensed a cord being severed between Nick and I. Such dreamy, half-conscious thoughts rolled across my mental landscape as I rolled back over, took a few deep breaths and floated off to sleep.

After the bad shroom trip, Nick grew subtly more and more ripe for consumption by Waverly, but I won't go too far into that here. He started getting swept down Waverly's rabbit holes, chasing down conspiracy theories online...Crystal Skulls, Enoch, child pedophiles...or some such nonsense. He became obsessed with shopping at Goodwill and other donation hubs, collecting all the literature the rest of society had abandoned to the garbage heaps. His lack of discernment and conspiratorial thinking grew alarming to me, though I had no words to vocalize it at the time.

experimental biology

I sensed my final confrontation with Waverly was close at hand, but attempted to carry on with daily life best I could. Because I had pushed it off, I ended up taking Biology 101 as a junior. So here I was, this lanky, smartass junior in with a bunch of freshmen. As the class took place around the lunch hour, I would regularly show up with Burger King to share. I made fast friends with a few of the underclassmen. I practically talked the ear off the girl in front of me, the cute brown-haired girl with glasses. I was a regular pain-in-the-ass, always borrowing pencils and distracting her and others from the lectures. Our instructor, Applewhite, was this sloppy fool who always smelled like an ashtray and a pot of coffee. He would shuffle around the room in his black orthopedic shoes, white-collared shirt half-untucked, sweating profusely, his body clearly protesting his life choices.

As is typical in biology, we dissected several creatures: worms, frogs, rats, etc. The formaldehyde stench made my mouth water and my stomach turn, my body's way of manifesting disgust. I had to walk away several times rather than vomit on the waxed tile floor. I wondered to myself where the school acquired these preserved creatures which we dissected in the name of science. While the dissections we're simultaneously interesting and gross, we grew bored and started hatching our own experiments.

The most notable of these started innocently enough, but soon took on a life of its own. At the prompting of a few bored freshmen, I began doing some pharmaceutical research on the instructor's tropical fish. They swam in two large tanks on the slate window sill, with a water filtration system humming away between them. One was a striped black and white variety with a yellow tail. The other was a shimmering blue with concentric white circles across its side. The shining, iridescent fish carved circles back and forth in the tank compulsively. The more I contemplated the regularity of this small, absurdly confining watery world, the more it began to bother my teenage brain. A new variable must be added to this perfect little world inside the glass.

One mundane high school day, a few freshman and I peered into the tank before class, staring at the beautiful caged creatures. The kid beside me produced some Ibuprofen from his pocket, offering the blue capsules in his open palm. I snatched them up and threw them in the filter tank.

"Only one way to find out."

"Quick," said the others, bolting back to their seats, "before Applewhite comes back."

Throughout class, the small group that was privy to the experiment eyed the fish periodically, out of the corner of their eyes. We waited. Nothing happened. The next day, we repeated the procedure. More eyes began watching the tank. Still nothing. We tried Tylenol. We waited.

This experiment continued for the better part of a week, with a wide variety of pills, before we got our first result. About a week into the experiment, the fish became aggressive. Abruptly, they would interrupt their smooth archs to dart and lash out at one another. It started slow. First a peck here, a nip there. The next day, we continued the medication. In the middle of a lecture, one boy raised his hand.

"Yes Michael," Mr. Applewhite prompted.

"This is a little off topic, but are your fish supposed to be attacking each other?"

We looked over at the tank. There was an all-out fish-fight occurring in the tank. The flabby, sweaty man set down his chalk and wandered over to the tank.

"Hmm. That is really strange," he said, peering through his thick glasses down into the churning waters of the tank.

"These fish are not known to have aggressive tendencies. I'll have to do some research."

Several of us exchanged knowing glances. I looked down at the brown tile floor, feeling half-guilty, half-intrigued. We were too far in to quit.

We administered the last dose that next day. The fish began to fall apart. Skin flapped off of them, in the current of the tankwater. Gaping holes appeared in their sides. Applewhite became distraught, wringing his hands and feeling helpless with his textbook knowledge of aquatic behavior. I don't know why we kept it up. Perhaps it was just something to break up the monotony. Perhaps we were genuinely intrigued by a living experiment. Perhaps we were just apathetic and numb by that point. Who knows? Not one of my proudest moments. Looking back, it seems incomprehensible to me that we could be so cruel to those fish or to that instructor, who most likely did not have much going for himself outside of the high school walls. Remembering his sad stares into that empty tank does bring up a pang of guilt, even now. I can't justify our cruelty.

An investigation was launched into the Case of the Aquatic Mishap. Individuals in the class were questioned. My name came up, as did the names of several others. Applewhite went down the list, interrogating each of us separately. I sat across the black slate table from that unfortunate man in a black t-shirt, "Zero" printed in large silver letters across my chest. My baggy pants, overinflated like my ego, flapped against my skinny, teenage chicken legs. I played with the chain attached to my wallet. To each of the instructor's questions, I was the most surprised and empathetic person in the world. I don't know if he bought my act, or just saw that questioning us was a lost cause, but suspicion evaporated and life inside the walls of Waverly High returned to relative normality.

I was hungry for meaning and pushing my limits. That "Zero" t-shirt reflected what I felt as I was pushed through the system of indoctrination. I was nothing, or at least nothing but an animal being pushed through a system that taught people to think and feel in efficient and predictable ways. The Smashing Pumpkins sang the song I advertised as I sat in front of that Bio 101 teacher, as I swam in my high school tank. Even the band's name said what we felt in those days: smashing pumpkins - destroying the fruits of the garden, smashing a fruitful harvest. For what? To lash back at the absurd predictability of our teenage lives, to demand real life experience - not second-hand knowledge. Adrenaline - she was all we thought we had in those days. And while curiosity might kill cats, as well as the occasional fish, it kept us alive. Such were the siren songs that filled my high school head. In that song and others, Billy Corgan vocalized what others and I felt. In the name of our high hopes, we cleaned up our reality, just to discover that it is empty and lonely...Waverly's version of religious mania. We end up intoxicated with madness, wanting more. We were being taught that despite all our rage, we were just rats in a cage, fish in a tank.

Thanks for the advice, Billy...and as you suggested, I did save my prayers for when I really needed them.

a grave man

Forrest Gump was buried in my parents' backyard… Well, to be more accurate, the remains of the man behind the myth rested about half a mile off, across an open field, past a lonely log cabin. The cemetery was a quiet burial ground, perched atop the ridge. Tall, stately green arbs and cypress reached up toward the sky, from among the stone markers. These thriving trees fed off clusters of nutrients below the surface, housed in rotting wooden boxes, tucked carefully into the ground by odd two-legged creatures.

We proceeded through the beige posts on either side of the entrance, past the black wrought iron fence. We continued down paths of crushed limestone that curved this way and that, meandering without rhyme or reason. On lazy days, we sometimes walked among the planted stones, inspecting names and dates. We smoked with the souls who had taken up residence there. Though we could be a rowdy bunch at times, the hush of Gump's grave neighbors inspired reflection and reverence in us.

I consider myself fortunate to have witnessed the many moods of this strange and silent place, one of Waverly's fair fields of friends, enemies, and strangers. On the sunny days, the long shadows cast by the green pillars stretched out across the plots, shifting throughout the day like a woodhenge as we slowly spun past the sun. This sunny day routine mimicked the shadowy living memories of those who now rested with the roots.

During the summer night, throughout all phases of the moon, crickets sang songs which echoed off the stones. On misty or fog-laden days, the graveyard took on an eerie, other-worldly appearance. Wisps and tufts of fog wove their way among the trees and stones, attempting to read the foreign language etched into granite, which had been mined and sold for remembrance. Sheets of mist watered the lush lawn blanket. Hard, driving rains gradually washed even names into the thirsty earth. Occasionally candles and colorful fresh-cut flowers graced the tiny little stone altars, turning the lonely stones into shrines of ancestor worship.

From the west entrance, the Gump plot sat at the far left hand corner of the cemetary - the northeast corner. In the book and film, Gump's sweetheart, Jenny, was sifted out from a sordid scene, plucked up by Forrest, set apart for a greater purpose. It turns out her actual name was Minnie - like the mouse. Her plain gravestone stood silent and upright, next to his.

The father of a boyhood friend also lay there among the fallen, tucked in, safe and sound, for a long night's sleep. Sometimes I saw his mother there, bringing blooms to lace the stone. Her new husband looked on in silence, sometimes squeezing her shoulder in solidarity. Some might say they were there for a visit with the past. Some might say they were gazing far off, into the future.

While strolling through this grave sight, questions often floated, like clouds across our minds. How much like Tom Hanks was the real Forrest? How many races had he really run? How do we foster that innocent openness which led to his full life and wealth of experience? How much of Jenny's personality and problems with addiction really rested in the ground with Minnie? How much was Hollywood hype? ...Is this where the fruits of our ambition come to rest? How do we confront the indifference of time and nature with confident expectation?

Forrest had served his country, run his race. Now we picked up the baton. In that monumental garden, we observed short life spans, and long, wondering at the stories hidden there.

my bay of pigs

I figure that, in all this, I should tell you what finally prompted me to pick up the pen - I mean, what really gave me the confidence to start writing in a structured format.

Waverly's guidance department had placed me in basic English, since I was a known troublemaker, with unremarkable grades. After a few weeks of worksheets and other busywork, I, with the assistance of my parents, informed my guidance counselor that her original guidance was mis-guided. I explained how she should have considered why I caused trouble, rather than that I caused trouble. It came down to the fact that I craved first-hand knowledge, and the busywork of basic English only drove me further into the depths of boredom. Academic English Lit was at least one step closer to something worth my time. So it was that my guidance counselor reluctantly placed me in Academic English.

A short, fiery woman welcomed me into her class. Mrs. Harbinger, the sign by the door read. Her blazing red hair was cropped close to her head. As she spoke, she motioned to me with her glasses, a glint in her eyes, a crafty smile on her face. Several clean-cut students eyed me with suspicion as I entered the room and found a seat in the back corner. My baggy jeans and heavy metal t-shirts were not what they expected to see in an academic classroom. I don't remember everything we read, but I know we read some Poe, which fired my imagination. While there were still occasional days of boredom, I got on fairly well in that class. A girl with loose light brown curls welcomed me into this new world. Tracy Galbraith was the daughter of a local judge. I couldn't have foreseen at that point we would date extensively once I had cleaned up and returned from military school. Harbinger challenged us, and, to my surprise, solicited my thoughts on texts. I remember debating her one afternoon over why so much American literature was so damn depressing. I don't remember reading one piece of comedy, or even satire. There were group projects, for which I went to Tracy's house. I was adept at dissecting literature thanks to my years in Catholic school, where all English was academic English and I had some phenomenal instructors.

There were occasional hiccups in my performance. I would knock out, slothlike some days. Especially those following my all-night Lucy benders. Lucy squeezes the juice from your brain, squeezes out the images as if wringing out a sponge.

Once I awoke to the whole class singing happy birthday to me, and cheering. Confusion washed over me - to wake up, out of a sound sleep, to a birthday song? *It wasn't my fucking birthday. What the hell was going on?* Harbinger's face rippled like a smiling wax mask as I sat up and gradually reassembled my immediate surroundings. The creaking cogs of my mind attempted to gain traction in this watery world. I was peering up, from the deep end of the pool, trying to make sense of the nonsensical. My stomach ached with gut-rot, that terrible churning discomfort that stemmed from ingesting chemicals it wasn't designed to ingest...

The last I remember of Harbinger's course was a research project. I wasn't too hyped about having to do research, and I struggled to hammer something out. Harbinger sat me down, started to question me about my pastimes. Soon we were on the topic of music, and then bands I followed, and then some of the political metal to which I listened. We landed on the band Machine Head. And then on the song "Bay of Pigs." Harbinger encouraged me to research this tropical bay on the southern coast of Cuba, and its role in American foreign policy. She encouraged me to analyze Machine Head's stance on U.S. foreign policy, and how effectively they communicated that stance. I dove into the crystal blue waters of that bay alongside the soldiers who America trained to invade their own country. I ran up onto the sand, past the intermittent palms with them as they were mowed down by communist machine gun fire. I dove into the national embarrassment when this operation failed and the truth came out. I dissected the lines in Machine Head's song. This experience was entirely new for me - the self-guided research, and an adult who was willing to dive into controversial episodes of American history alongside me. Harbinger encouraged me to pursue what I loved - something that most adults at the time didn't seem too concerned about.

Harbinger probably deserves a huge chunk of the credit for convincing me that institutions could be salvaged, rather than torn apart, if the right people were in the right places. She probably deserves a huge chunk of the credit for the fact that I now teach both History and English. In those late hours of my junior year, as my time with Waverly waned, she planted many seeds which wouldn't sprout until long after the smoldering remains of my adolescent ego had washed into the soil.

the sleepwalkers

At one of the final full-moon parties out at Scatterfield Ranch, I had thrust my hand deep into a tub of beer and what did I find, but an icy pint of Jose Cuervo! I twisted the top, breaking the seal, cheersed Jacqueline, who was close at hand, and took a long swig. My throat burned and the taste of tequila danced on my tongue. I offered the bottle to her, which she gently grabbed without hesitation. Pulling her straight, firy hair behind her ears, she tipped the bottom toward the stars and sipped for a minute or so. Her throat contracted as she took down a few gulps. Her raised jawline appeared to me soft and pure as we stood there under a street lamp in that gravel drive. She passed it back to me and again I drank. She raised a rust-colored eyebrow in my direction and smirked.

"That's quite the find. Let's keep it to ourselves. Walk with me," she suggested, motioning for me to follow her across the dark front yard.

I followed, stepping off the gravel drive into the fresh-cut grass with her.

"You ever get sick of this place, Jay?...Indiana....Do you ever want to just get the hell out?...hop in the car and not look back?"

"Of course, Jacquie," I agreed, emphatically. "Every day. Who can live like this for the rest of their lives," I motioned around, indicating the quiet house at our left and the distant sound of voices off across the yard.

I gestured with the half-empty bottle. She took a sip and passed it back. We reached a mowed trail at the far side of the yard, leading off into a grassy field, which was dotted here and there with volunteer scrub trees. We continued off down the trail, walking side-by-side. She looped her arm around mine.

"I want to find a liberal school, up on the Great Lakes...study activism, or social justice, or something with a little soul in it..."

"Yeah, if you're looking for a little soul, you're not going to find it around here. Wasn't your dad in that Doctors Without Borders program?"

"He was," she smiled over at me. "Maybe that's where I get it...it's in my blood...What are you going to do Jay?"

"Not sure. Maybe something in music...Definitely not stay here," I laughed.

She stepped into a dip and almost lost her balance. I tugged her back toward me, and we careened, laughing down the path. I had to skip a step so that we were again in sync.

"How far does this trail go," she wondered aloud.

"Umm, it zig-zags all over...maybe half a mile...piggyback ride?" I asked, crouching so she could hop on my back.

She threw her arms around my neck and hopped her legs up to squeeze my waist, so that she was straddling me. I looped my arms beneath her legs for support, adjusted her weight, and set off further down the trail.

"You reading anything right now?" she asked, in my ear, kind of turning me on.

"Just a bio of Jim Morrison," I laughed, her hair now tickling my neck.

"You?"

"*On the Road*," she said breathily, too close to my ear.

"You would," I laughed, starting to jog and purposefully stumbling from one side of the trail to the other, so that she shifted unsteadily across my back.

I tripped on a stick, and then we went down laughing, into the tallgrass. She fumbled for my zipper, and I for hers. As she tugged the jeans down from my skinny hips, I felt the cool night air, and her warmth against me.

After fooling around for a time, we lay upon our backs in the grass, looking up at the sky, her hand still across my chest, and mine wrapped around her. At some point, we sat up and gradually finished off the Cuervo, continuing our conversation where we left off.

"Life is holy," she said, "and every moment precious...That's Kerouac."

"...lovers desperately try to fuse their insulated ecstasies into a single self-transcendence...Huxley."

Our intense stares met for a brief moment in the moonlight. We stood, reassembled ourselves, and continued down the path, which ended at the paved county road. We turned and kicked along through the coarse grass of the ditch near the road.

"Who do you have for English?" She asked.

"Harbinger. She's cool."

"I have Camfrey," she groaned. "Terrible. We haven't read one real book all year. Just textbook snippets. It's a fucking travesty."

At the corner, I went to swing around the street sign and, realizing it was loosely in the ground, jerked it up out of its hole. She shook her head and smirked again. We continued on back toward the party, side by side. I set the pace, using the street sign as a staff, like Moses headed down from the mountain.

When we re-emerged at the heart of the party, Red was standing atop a picnic table singing "Bawitdaba," some nonsense Kid Rock song.

Jacquie and I marched up to the fire, street sign in hand. Red called over to us,

"And they come bearing a sign!"

a bad moon rising

In the spring of my seventeenth year, I found myself at a party in the heart of Waverly. She had snuggled us up, lured us in with whiskey and her finest weed. The party was in a ground-level, mustard yellow apartment complex near the Comfort Suites hotel. Early evening hues still hovered in the air - pinks, blues, and purples - just after our mother star had snuggled up for the night.

My new cell phone - what I called my electronic leash - buzzed in my pocket. What now? I thought. I passed off the water bong to Sam. The music was too loud to hear the voice on the other end of the line, so I stepped outside to take the call. I recognized the number and fidgeted nervously as I stepped outside.

"Hell...Hello?" I stammered.

"You need to come home," dad said in his deep, matter-of-fact tone.

Damn curfew, I cursed to myself, looking out across the parking lot of the nearby hotel. *I'm not sober*, I wanted to say. But my parents had made it clear: drinking was not an option. In their opinion, partying was all or nothing. They would not give me permission to do something illegal.

"I'll take off soon," I said resignedly.

The call ended. A dial tone. I better take off before those Jack Daniels shots kick in, I thought to myself.

Thirty minutes later, my parents were slamming the door to the garage and frantically climbing in the car, peeling out as they raced down the drive.

I had just rolled their red van on a gravel road several miles west of Waverly. I was attempting to retrieve my cd player, which slid off the seat, when I lost control of the car. Tires slid across the loose gravel as a foot punched on the brake. The speeding van crashed through a mailbox, sailed up an embankment, and went airborne. The vehicle crashed back down onto the gravel road, upside-down, facing the direction it was originally headed when right-side-up. But now the van resembled a crushed, incapacitated insect.

The clock calmly showed 12:13 across the LED display, into the darkness. My parents began to scour the country roads, in search of the van. Silence hung heavy between them, like the fog just outside the windows.

I phoned immediately after once again pushing up on the shattered glass littering the ceiling, unbuckling, and crawling out onto the dusty gravel. I let them know I had escaped the wreckage unharmed. I didn't want them to think Waverly had finally swallowed me up. I stood staring at the hissing metal remains of the van across this otherwise silent and fateful night.

My parents sped toward the location I mentioned on the call - a vague approximation of where I thought I was. My dad drove up and down the road, yet saw nothing out of the ordinary. My mom's fingernails clenched the armrests so hard that imprints still remain to this day. Her eyes searched the dark, for any sign of her son. Her piercing gaze lept from shadow to shadow. My father's tired eyes were narrowed, and continued scanning the illuminated road ahead, as the headlights gradually revealed more and more gravel.

On their second pass through the area, they received a phone call from Waverly's finest, who directed them to the correct road, and the empty, smoldering remains of their wrecked vehicle.

When my parents finally arrived at the crash site, the flashing blue and red hue of squad car sirens eerily set the scene. Gradually, what remained of their vehicle came into view. The heap of glass, fiberglass, and metal lay upside down in the middle of the gravel road, completely obstructing it, a giant hurdle in their path.

My mother uttered a prayer to the Virgin Mary and wept silently. My father, for lack of words, simply stared at the smoking wreck, as if it were a metallic beast that trod across his path, now to be confronted. A tow truck with flashing yellow lights sat ready to haul the heap of metal up onto his truck, and away. The tow truck driver stood beside his truck, smoking a cigarette and calmly awaiting his cue.

A uniformed officer walked over to meet my parents and motioned for a man in a navy blue bathrobe, with matching house shoes, to come forward. The officer, with neatly slicked back and faded gray hair, patiently explained the presence of this blue-robed, effeminate man standing near the end of the driveway next to the smoking wreckage. The van had destroyed the robed fellow's mailbox and blocked his drive. The robed man explained, in a high, lisp-laden voice, he heard the crash as he sat watching television on his couch, winding down from a busy day at work. With careful, concerned steps, he had fluttered down to the end of his long drive to investigate the smash that interrupted the routine of his night.

"I just wanted to make sure no one was hurt," the robed figure said emphatically, gesturing with his hands, "but when I got to the end of the drive, all I found was this wrecked van.... No sign of a driver."

Tears again welled up in my mom's eyes as she explained to the robed man that I had called, explaining that I was unharmed. She now prayed this was actually the case. My father wrapped his arm around her in comfort and solidarity.

"I am not ready to lose Jay," she wept to the Waverly officer, as if anyone is ever ready to confront such a reality.

The officer spoke softly, saying that his men had searched the surrounding roads and found no sign of her son, but that they would keep up the search for several hours. My parents held each other and both prayed that their son was safe.

"For the record, to your knowledge, was your son under the influence of any substances?" asked the officer, pad in hand.

"I'm not sure," my father responded quickly, before my mother had a chance. "We know as much as you do right now."

The officer nodded and told them that they should go home in case their son had gotten a ride back. He told my parents to phone the department once I turned up, and then motioned to the tow truck driver.

All four of the onlookers watched in silence as what remained of the van was hauled up onto the tow truck and then driven off into the darkness. The screeches of the metal against metal grated still on my mother's shattered nerves. The patrol cars set off in either direction to continue the search along the backroads surrounding Waverly. My mother and father slowly opened their respective doors, climbed back in, and pulled off to await the arrival of their wayward son.

I had pushed up on the ceiling of the vehicle so I could release the safety belt which held me suspended upside down. A panicked sense of Deja Vu swept over me. I instinctively hurried through the broken window, avoiding what broken shards I could. After climbing from the smoking wreckage, I stared incoherently at the hissing pile of glass and metal, running my fingers through my locks. *Fuck. Double fuck*, I thought. It was as if I was seeing the world through a darkened glass. That crazy-haired hag of fate had blocked my path yet again, and in the process I demolished someone's mailbox.

Waverly spoke to me from the shadows, set off against the chirping crickets and mating frogs somewhere in the spring night.

"Come out and play," she said, in her raspy tones.

I couldn't see her face. It was hidden by her hood and wisps of wiry hair. I bent, scooping up handfuls of gravel. I hurled them into the darkness, at her unseen face.

"Come out and play…" She repeated, before melting into the surrounding blackness.

Trees lined the road in a dark and silent watch. Reluctantly I pulled out my cellular leash and placed a call to my parents, giving them a rough estimate of where I thought I was. A gravel road down which I had never driven before... Immediately upon ending the call, I began to consider the impending consequences of this damned hissing wreckage before me.

First, my mind went to what my parents would say - more and more disappointment added to the already mountainous pile. Then my thoughts churned around the legal repercussions. My mind began to generate a fictional gloss across the situation. Waverly's finest would arrive to find a "young Caucasian male" standing next to this hissing wreckage. Surely this would not bode well for my legal record. I would lose my license to commute, and God only knew what else. I had already been on probation. I realized I could not stand by and let it go down like that. I had to make one final effort.

I hurried through the trees which lined the ditch at the west side of the road. They scraped at my legs, but nonetheless welcomed me into their protective darkness. Though I did not know it at the time, a windy spirit watched closely over me. I set off in a northwesterly direction, in the direction of Waverly Road and my parents' house. This was a fifteen to twenty mile walk, but a sobering and moonlit one across the plowed fields. I knew that if I milked the time, if I took long enough, the cops would wait until the next day to come out and get a statement. I was buying time with careful footsteps. By morning, full sobriety would set in. I tread across freshly plowed earth of farm fields, watching my steps carefully in the moonlight. She lit my path, and seemed curious as to how this all would turn out.

As I made my way across the second of these fields, it occurred to me that keeping my phone wouldn't be good. I did not want to be distracted by frantic and worried calls. I did not want to be tracked or traced. I took the phone from my pocket, powered it down, and flung it into the darkness of the field. I crossed tilled field after tilled field, ready to be planted. Thankfully it had been a dry spring, so the dirt clods crunched under my steps rather than forcing me to slip and slide in a muddy mess.

At one point, I trod across a cow pasture with tall grass, where the stupefied cows stood, staring absently into the night. They turned their heads and watched this strange scene, this odd boy of the night as he strode diagonally across their field. They watched as he slipped between the strands of barbed wire and once again vanished.

Soon after, I came to a familiar crossroads and continued on in the direction of Waverly Road, taking to the country roads rather than the fields, which had become uneven and less inviting. For a time I walked in silence. Occasionally a lone car could be seen approaching a mile off in the distance. I would wait until they were closer and then dive off the road into the protective darkness of the grassy ditch. After the vehicle passed, I would resume my dark walk on the uneven country roads. I was one shadow in a world of fleeting shadows. I could feel the eyes of Waverly on the back of my neck. This was the closest she had ever been.

As I approached the main railroad bridge in the small adjacent town of Cadence, I thought it better to make my way down into the ravine and across the railroad tracks rather than risk strutting across the main bridge for anyone to see. Cadence was the cranky sister of Waverly, and I dared not awaken her. Her sleepy thorns and branches clawed at my arms and legs, scraped at my face, but I continued on across the tracks and up the other side, away from her stiff, thorny fingers.

I crossed a highway, which bordered the north edge of Cadence. I continued off into the fields along the opposite side - fields whose rolling hills stretched to cover the remaining four miles between myself and home. Sometimes taking to the road, sometimes to the field, I made my way up Waverly Road, occasionally jumping into the ditch as a car passed. I carried on full conversations with the waning moon, which graciously lit my path. I kissed her hand and feverishly thanked this friend for lighting my way. I then began pouring all my thoughts and worries out to her. She ran her fingers through my coarse brown hair, calming anxious thoughts. Tears began to flow, dropping down onto the asphalt. So many tears streamed forth that I had trouble seeing the road ahead. The moon threw down her tears as well, so that I almost slipped and fell. Each time, she caught me in her gentle hands, and wiped my fears away.

Assorted scenarios played out in my mind as I approached the looming, but well-lit, fortress. I took a deep breath, pressed the doorbell and waited, blowing a kiss to the moon from the doorstep. She and I parted ways. My parents ran and embraced me as they opened the door. Tears of joy were shed for health and safety. Then reasons were sought, to explain away this insane event. From somewhere inside me spewed out the most confusing and disjointed story I could concoct. My parents stared as if I had just carried out a verbal abortion, and there the thing sat in front of them...bits and pieces of the night...giving a stranger a ride...some kind of medicine...the stranger at the wheel…

All these snippets took on a life of their own, whirling around in front of me, demonic and monstrous, pulling and tugging at the facial expressions of my parents in strange and terrible ways. Questions began to fly about the room like bats, scooping up the insects of the air, swerving erratically about. Additional chunks of disjointed information began to fall from my moving mouth. The faces of my parents shifted from relief and disappointment to confusion and horror as these strange bits and pieces of truth, lie, and chaos commingled, and dripped from my tortured tongue.

My parents were so confused and tired, that they ended the questioning not long after it started. They quickly saw that they would never get a straight answer to the questions they asked. They told me to go take a shower, and then to get some rest. Meanwhile, they phoned the Waverly Police Department to let them know that I was safe. Dispatch told them she would send someone out the next day to take a statement. I finished showering and drank what felt like an ocean. I slept the most sound sleep I had ever slept in my life. All the fight, and all the flight had been drained from my sleepy frame. I knew the war was over.

like an unoiled machine

The gold-plated sign on the door read, "A. Hecklesworth, Public Defender". I had been marched warily through that giant wooden door by my parents. The havoc had finally gone too far, and I sat in an uncomfortable chair awaiting my fate.

All cases that came out of Waverly were handled in Mount Comfort, the county seat. I could feel Waverly waiting in the wings, her hot breath of vengeance upon my neck. Her numb eyes narrowed, and her fingers fidgeted, as she contemplated into which of the juvenile detention centers I would be cast.

I sat, idly watching drool form at the corners of an ancient mouth, and waited for the drops of spittle to ride gravity down, onto the stacks of tan case files that littered the desk. The mountains of paper rose up on all sides of this Mr. Hecklesworth. I imagined him lording over those mountains like the ignorant and angry old testament god. Perhaps the slobber would splash into a valley between the stacks, wrinkling the dry and dusty papers there...But at the last second, he sucked it back up into his over-salivated jowls.

All of this was taking place beneath a bulbous red nose, the size and shape of Louisiana. He shook his enormous, heavy head to keep himself awake. A stubby finger poked the glasses back up onto the bridge of his boot-shaped nose. He wheezed slightly, and when he did so, the long grey nose hairs shuttered in the wind. Tufts of white hair lined a bald patch at the center of his cranium. I eyed this hunched figure curiously, this terrible trivium, this bucolic creature birthed of bureaucracy. I continued to study him. I had seen bureaucratic animals before, but never one of such advanced age. Ten slow minutes had passed. I analyzed the concentric brown circles his coffee mug painted across the papers and folders near his wrinkled right hand.

My parents and I waited as he ploddingly read over my charges. My father looked down at his watch, and then over at me. I shrugged my shoulders and raised my eyebrows, as if to say, "How long are we going to do this?" My mother looked out the window, wishing she was outside the stuffy concrete walls of this government building. My father cleared his throat and started to speak. The creature immediately raised one finger, signaling for him to wait. This was the fastest we had seen the creature move. I was slightly surprised by the swift raising of that wrinkled finger. I ran my fingers through my shoulder-length hair. Five more minutes passed.

I knew my father was ready to jump out of his seat. He's an impatient man, brimming with ceaseless agitation. A blue vein pulsed on the side of his temple. His impatience became palpable, and flowed out into the stuffy, humid air.

You see, my father industriously oversees the construction of schools, airports, hospitals, and stadiums. Time is money to him, and I could tell he resented this slow, incompetent creature for trodding across his path. My father looked at his watch again. Finally, the creature coughed and started to speak.

"Your son," he started, haltingly, "...is being charged with leaving the scene of a property damage accident?"

His eyes lolled up to meet my father's, and then over to my mother's. I think I was invisible to his ancient eyes. Perhaps this strange creature was only able to see adults?

"We know the charges!" My father burst in frustration. "What we're here to find out is what you plan on doing to defend our son against those charges. You are a public defender, are you not?"

The hunched creature again looked down at the stack of papers in front of him. I imagined him shuffling through them, as if they were a giant deck of cards. Abruptly, the heavy lids closed. The creature began to snore.

"Are you fucking serious?" My father spat, outraged.

I started to laugh. The absurdity was too much for my young mind. My mother wrung her hands and looked flustered.

"Tom, watch your language," she chastised my father.

"I think my language is the least of our damn problems," he said, gesturing at the sleeping embodiment of public defense.

"Let's go!" My father motioned for my mom and I to get up. "This is ludicrous. We are not wasting any more of our time here. We need a real attorney if we are going to have our way with those bloodthirsty prosecutors!"

We rose and followed my father out into the hall. I am afraid you will think I am over-exaggerating. I am not. That was the end of our experience with public defenders. We found out later that the idiot died the next week. I would venture that the world is better with one less "public defender".

Why we even went to the meeting with that old fool, I'll never know. I have four attorneys in my family. Maybe my dad was too embarrassed by my actions to ask the family for help. Maybe he was too proud? Maybe he was trying to save some money? At any rate, we met with a real attorney who had been referred to us by a family friend. This new attorney had an office on the square in Waverly. He didn't take my case, but acted as a mediator with the judge to get the precise sentence my parents wanted: court-ordered completion of a 15-month Behavior Modification Program - a military school which specialized in brainwashing young adults between the ages of 12 and 18. I wasn't surprised.

My parents had been mentioning drastic options in recent days.

Four choices were given: Costa Rica, Jamaica, Mexico, or Montana...I wanted to stay in the country. God only knew what went on across the border, far away from watchful eyes. I flipped through the glossy brochures. Each was checkered with photos and captions, touting the amenities on the respective facilities. Who knew what went on in those facilities outside the U.S.? I picked up the Montana brochure. "Crooked Timber Creek Academy" advertised the rustic font. Cabins, mountains, and an expansive lake graced the cover. I peeled it open to read blurbs on hiking, horseback riding, river-rafting, and team-building exercises. While I sensed that there was a bit of false advertising at play, I nonetheless gambled on Montana.

My parents were not about to let me get chewed up in the system, but they wanted me to learn from my heedless actions. Who wouldn't want the same for their kid? I feel for those who don't have the social or financial resources to fight for justice on behalf of their kids. But in our system, only the middle class get justice. I don't know how to fix the system, but I do know that "justice as fairness" is a long way off for those without the cash, if my run-in with public defense is any indication.

The program at Crooked Timber Creek promised to modify my behavior, to reshape me into a "productive member of society". *What was I? A malfunctioning cog in the machine?* The judge consented. A court order was issued.

So I went about my cloudy, bittersweet last days in Waverly. I withheld the news from her as long as possible, so as not to see her wistful anger bubble to the surface. Where I was headed, I would be out of her reach, beyond the sway of her manipulation. I knew the news wouldn't sit well with her. She wouldn't stomach it. I felt her clingy hands reaching out in my direction, and a shiver went up my spine. I was no longer her hope, her toy, or her experiment. Something much larger had expanded the protective sheild around me. I was not yet sure what it could be, but I now knew I was not destined to waste away in Waverly's hands.

outside looking out

All my antics had run their course. All the tricks of my idle hands had been tried. As I packed my suitcase in preparation for this fateful new phase, Waverly came imploringly to me. Her pleading, vampiric eyes would haunt me for years to come.

"Run away, Jay... Stay with me." Her babbling brook begged. "I see your future. If you leave, you'll come back changed. You'll come back a sell-out, a yuppie, a hipster, or worse yet, a snob."

I felt the hot wind issuing forth from her park of deathstones, and backed instinctively away. I looked into the desperate, pleading eyes near her green and watery forest. At a gut level, I felt her sapping energy from me.

"I'm tired, Waverly" I sighed. "I need some rest. I will change, but I won't sell out." I no longer had the energy for deliberation. All the fight was gone.

Waverly had drained much drink from my neck by that late stage. And I began to see her as a pale and pathetic parasite, feeling the traumatic separation from its host. Neither of us had reckoned that she wouldn't be the one to finally tie my idle hands.

She reached down and squeezed me tightly and desperately one last time, and then walked dejectedly back into her haunted and lonely life. I watched her go, a wisp of dust-colored hair floating behind her down the dirt road. I continued staring after her, lost in thought, the sun perched low on the horizon.

I have a grainy photo of myself and the Scatterfield boys from that last day of freedom. The photo was taken at the end of my parents' sidewalk. The guys and I form an arc, with Nick and I at the center between Red and Jack. A baggy purple and black Coal Chamber t-shirt clings to my skinny frame. The fact is that I had very little coal in my metaphorical chamber by that point. Some said that great pressure could turn coal to diamonds. I had my doubts. I left hoping the crew could ward off Waverly's advances, that somehow I was the lucky one for getting out while I could.

I had attempted to break free from my shell, throwing myself against the

Waverly's small world. She had grown increasingly desperate. With reluctance, I kissed my addictions goodbye, as a child who gives up his favorite toy. I wanted to follow up on those agreements I had made before stepping onto this plane of existence, I really did. The time was now, I sensed it.

Many would have wagered that Jay Chapparal wouldn't make it out of Waverly in one piece, wouldn't live to tell the tales. Waverly had a headstone with my name upon it. Every now and then she flipped it in the air, as if tossing a coin. It could be said that Waverly stacked the cards against me, but gradually I found my way back to the One who made those very cards, the One who could change their face value at a moment's notice.

I'd respect your point of view if you said that was horseshit. I might feel that way too, if I hadn't been tugged from the jaws of Waverly so many times. In what way was I different from any of the others Waverly hungrily consumed? I was an outsider - that's all that I could gather. I had necessary points of comparison which allowed me to see through Waverly's lies…My pale hands ached from their idle work in Waverly.

I stared through my reflection in the clear glass of my bedroom window, north across the grassy fields, at nothing in particular. "The Winds of Change," by the Scorpions, played in the background. The icy winds of the North were coming, bringing trouble and change.

My grayish blue eyes surprised even me with their deep sadness. Waverly sapped the light from my eyes. Sideburns stretched down the sides of my face toward my chin, framing my taut features. The shifting winds of my fateful circumstances had me all fucked up at present. I went into the bathroom, pulled my shirt up over my head, took out the clippers, and began to cut off my dreadlocks, which fell one by one onto the countertop and floor with sad thuds. I wouldn't give them the pleasure of humiliating me by forcing me down and cutting my hair. My mother had a fire burning on the hearth. I fed those dreads to the hungry flames, watching as they shriveled and burned down to nothing. Then I lathered up my face and shaved the sideburns, my pride swirling down the drain.

The next morning we rose early for the drive to Chicago. From there, we would fly into Spokane, Washington. I stumbled through the whole process in a daze, as one walking to the gallows. Resignation muted me. So many unknowns...So many faces, all living different lives. My dad picked up the keys to the rental car from the kiosk. Mom and I retrieved the checked suitcases from the baggage claim. We all climbed into the crimson Buick sedan and pulled off toward Bigfork, Montana.

The road out of Spokane proper gradually ushered us into rolling hills, farms, and evergreen mountain forests. I reached over and lowered the window, letting the fresh air blast me in the face. Dad looked back at me in the rearview and I avoided his eyes, gazing out the window instead. I'd never smelled air that fresh, a million christmas trees issuing forth their balsam scent to ease my troubled mind. This was a little bit of alright. Music was flowing up into my ears through my ear buds. Dave Matthews Band - "Typical Situation." I started to sense my perspective shifting, as if the land itself was welcoming me, hugging me to her breast. With such scenery and such scents, what did it matter what trials I had in store? A carpet of pines stretched out across the sleeping rock formations, as far as I could see. A sense of meaning beyond comprehension, certainty without knowledge, washed over me. And I knew I was exactly where I was "supposed" to be, as surely as I knew I was in a car, headed east at 65 mph.

The chords of the song seemed a soundtrack for the moment. I'd heard this song a thousand times, but seemed to be really hearing it for the first time now. Evergreens continued to comb through my consciousness, as I took in the rugged slopes. While I had an acute sense of being rejected by my family and my society, I for the first time felt as if I was being welcomed by something much greater than all of that. I ran my fingers across the plush fabric of the back seat, smoothing patterns in the different directions the threads lay.

We snaked our way through the mountains and down into Bigfork. We pulled up to a motel covered in thick slats of cedar siding. We emerged from the car and stretched. After removing the luggage that we'd packed for this single night in town and getting things settled in the room, my dad announced he was heading down to the Flathead River for a swim. His blue towel was draped over his shoulder. His chubby belly created a slight bulge above the waistband of his teal swim trunks. He asked me if I cared to join him. I declined. My mom knocked on the door to my room, and then peeked in.

"Phone," she said, holding it up for me to grab. "I'm going down to the water to watch your father."

I nodded.

"Hullo?" I chimed.

"You know you don't have to go, Jay" Brett started. "If you can make it from Montana to Colorado, you know I could arrange to put you up until you get on your feet here."

"I know, I know. Believe me, I have considered it! ...But I would have to stay off the radar for years. It would get old real quick. I'm tired of running, tired of hiding. Besides, if I ever want to go to college, I can't pay for that on my own. I will need their help."

"I hope you're right, my friend," warned Brett. "It just seems so crazy that your folks would have you locked up for flipping their car. People make mistakes. It's not like you killed someone. You ran over someone's mailbox and left a car upside down. Serves them right for being so uptight."

"I know, I know, I know. But as much as I'm not crazy about this whole setup, running is a very short term solution. The camp has to be better than jail. Otherwise, why would they try so hard to keep me out of the juvie and insist on shipping me off to this place?"

"I really hope you're right," Brett came back hesitantly. "But in case it doesn't work out, the offer is always on the table. No orange jumpsuit. No cabin in the woods. Just a new home in Golden, Colorado..."

"Well, at any rate, it's beautiful out here, man. You should smell the mountain air. Never breathed fresher, cleaner air in my life! Even beats Colorado. These pine woods and this big sky put me at ease."

"Hahaha...well you're a little more optimistic than I would be in your shoes. Some of those camps are worse than jail. I hope you stashed a weapon of some sort...And don't come back as some sort of short-haired, preppy, brainwashed SOB."

"Of course, man! I have a blade sealed up inside my shampoo bottle. There's no way they'll dump that. I'm required to bring in those toiletries...If I think I need it, I will bust it out while I am showering. 'I'll drop him like a toilet seat, Tommy!'" I joked, quoting one of Brett's favorite taekwondo films. "You really have no faith in me if you think I'll come back all prepped-out!"

"Hahaha...well good luck to your crazy ass! Hopefully you won't need it! You always seem to find a way to make it work. Hit me up when you are on the other side!"

"Will do, man. Peace."

"Peace."

Other than seeing a moose cross the railroad tracks and wander into town, the rest of the evening passed uneventfully, and I slept like a rock. The next morning, at a little Ma and Pa restaurant, I attempted to consume a cinnamon roll the size of my face. After dad paid for breakfast, we climbed into the crimson sedan and headed toward the edge of town. We turned onto Blue Shale Road.

I thought to myself that "road" was a generous term for what was really a glorified dirt path, curving precariously along the pine-clad mountain. Undoubtedly, it was an old logging trail. One wrong move would send the vehicle cascading down the mountainside, across the blueish grey shale which paved the mountain wall down to the sleepy river, giving the road its name.

Dad turned onto a gravel driveway near a wooden sign which read "Crooked Timber Creek Academy" in white lettering against a green background. Below the name of the school was engraved the image of a lone wolf, howling at the woods beyond. As we wound our way onto the facility proper, I saw lines of kids marching in formation, criss-crossing the campus. Giant two-story cabins came into view and I sensed that a new adventure was brewing, one unlike anything I'd ever known.

dedications

I dedicate this book to the Great Spirit, the prodigal God that allows us the freedom to choose, and welcomes us back when our self-serving errands inevitably fail.

I also dedicate this collection to all the adults who helped lead me through the valley of the shadow of death. I truly would not be here today without you.

I dedicate these tales to those who lost their lives in the struggle.

Lastly, I dedicate this book to my students and all those searching for meaning amid what might seem to be chaos in the moment. Keep searching. Stay up.

May the Great Spirit bless you and keep you. May the face of God shine upon you.